The Broken Prince

Kara Linaburg

Kara Linaburg

Book cover design: Kairos Book Design And
Editing

www.thebeautifullybrokenblog.com

We are all broken. That's how the light gets in.
Ernest Hemingway

To the ones who feel alone in the fight. I wrote this for you. And for my readers who have loved on me for so long. You are the reason I love to write.

Kara Linaburg

Prologue

The Seer's words always came to pass. When he uttered the dreams that attacked his peaceful sleep, when he spoke of the visions that plagued the quiet, they never failed to come into being.

When he'd told old man Arvid that his wife would betray him for another man if he didn't treat her with more respect, two summers later Arvid found himself alone in his hut with only his mutt to keep him company.

When the Seer had predicted that Erik would be killed by the king's soldiers, the following day Erik's head was on a spike for whispering lies about Sindaleer's ruler.

But it wasn't just little happenings that Falk predicted that made the folk take notice. He'd known when Thayer was planning his attack, long before any of the Sindaleerians had guessed their home was to be invaded. Three summers before a lord with a growing army declared war on Sindaleer, Falk predicted: "A man from the Dark Isles will come, a leader who fears the specially Gifted, and will in turn make them the most feared species in the land. I see his face in my sleep, and rest evades knowing what he plans for our country. Our Gifteds will be branded and killed, feared above any other folk. Our elders will be beheaded and new ones will take their place. Our lads will become his toy soldiers and the widows will die of hunger."

The folk laughed at the Seer, calling him a crazy young man who was taking his Gifting as a teller of doom too seriously.

And yet, all that he foretold fell into place, each prediction one by one. Lord Thayer, with his crafty tongue to persuade the masses, invaded Sindaleer with his blood-thirsty army. The X was branded on Falk's wrists, marking him a feared Gifted, and slowly he turned into a hermit, moving further and further into the wood, an outcast to his folk.

But not before he made one final prediction: "Thayer's bastard son will claim the proceeding throne, and the maiden of fire he marries will carry on the bloodline. Because of your ignorance, the generations of the hated Thayer will continue. Beware folk of Sindaleer. Because you laughed at prophecy, you will now live under the thumb of one you hate until you perish."

The folk came at Falk, threatening to behead him where he stood, and the man fled, escaping to the Lowleen Forest.

But someone took heed of his warning. A young

woman with dark hair and hard eyes that saw the world beyond her years. She'd felt the agony of death that Thayer and his army had left in their wake, and at Falk's words, she vowed that they would never come to pass.

She would murder King Thayer herself, if that is what it took, killing the foretold maiden and anyone who tried to extend the line of Thayer.

"May the blood of my son and husband be on my hands if I do not have my revenge," she whispered.

I

The fields around Serena's village of Aedre glistened under the sun's touch. Through the one window of her little cottage, she watched the men come in early from the corn fields, and the elders as they made their way to the community lodge to begin preparations for the Ceremony. Little children chased one another around thatched huts, their laughter mingling with the chatter of the women as they rekindled their dying fires to prepare for the feast.

The transition from summer to autumn brought cold weather, storytellings with the elders, and thick frost on thatched roofs. But autumn also brought the air of change and the most anticipated moment of the year: the annual Ceremony of Elect.

Lads would become men, legends would be retold, and the young ones would dance around the fire, the festivities lasting long into the night. The moon would climb the sky, turning a milky white as the beat of the drums pulsed through the earth.

Moving away from the window, Serena fixed her attention on her own dying fire at the center of the one-room cottage. Out of habit, she glanced over her shoulder as if someone stood in the shadows watching her.

She could never be too careful.

Bending down, she closed her eyes, allowing warmth to steal into her body, seeping through her skin like sunlight. She studied her outstretched hand, the orange glow illuminating her sun-tanned skin, soaking under her nails. Little tongues of fire appeared, hovering above her fingertips.

With a flick, she sent them into the wood, before digging her nails into her palm. The flames on her fingertips extinguished, but the wood before her came back to life.

Her Mam's voice sounded in her head.
"Ye shouldn't be making fire, Serena. Ye know the king outlawed the use of Gifts when he took over the land. Don't put yeself in danger. Ye have Hunter to take care of."

"I know, Mam," Serena whispered. *But ye bore the Marks too.*

The king of Sindaleer had divided his folk since the beginning of his reign, filling them with fear for those different from themselves.

As a Gifted, one had magical-like abilities possessed at birth that did not come about from spells or witchcraft. For many years, the Gifteds were seen as no

9

different from other folk, none lower than the other. But that changed when King Thayer had claimed the throne.

He'd feared the Gifted folk with talent and skill beyond his own, and branded them, proclaiming that any Gifted and Marked who used their Gift, would be killed.

The fear of her kind had grown over the years, and now, with the change of times, folk would see her as a threat if they knew of the fire that flowed through her veins. Death would claim her if they learned of the flames she created, of what she created in secret when the door of her cottage closed.

Enough of these gloomy thoughts. Serena stood, crossing over to the wash basin to splash lukewarm water on her face and neck. The tattooed X's on her wrist caught the light in the broken piece of Reflection. Da had once bought the Reflection from traders of the Seas for Mam, making the other village women jealous of such a prize.

The droplets clung to her chin and eyelashes, and she blinked as they slid down her face and neck. She took a scrap of fabric from the table and rubbed her skin dry, hanging the wet cloth on the hook above the Reflection.

Her excitement for the evening grew as she fried bread dough in the lard over the fire. Soon her brother would be standing in front of her, home, safe and sound. She could cut his hair one last time—the strands the color of a red summer's sunset, the only proof that he had been adopted.

She would give him his new moccasins that he would wear to his soldier training in a month's time, and they would recount stories together as the sun died. For one last time.

Because, unlike in the fairy tales they loved as children, here in the country of Sindaleer, only miles from the capitol, happy endings did not exist.

Looping her thumbs through the round holes at the cuff of her dress's sleeves, Serena ensured her tattooed wrists remained invisible to prying eyes, before flipping the fried bread into the basket on the table.

Hunter would soon be gone once more, but unlike his previous thirty-day trip to prove his manhood, this time it would be for good. She ignored the lump settling in her throat, telling herself to be happy for him.

He would no longer have association with Serena, his quiet sister of the country of Sindaleer whom everyone pitied. She was too shy, too quiet, kept to herself too much for anyone to really bother.

But they didn't know she harbored a secret, one that she struggled to keep with each passing day. A secret that both burdened and frightened her.

"Serena."

She whirled around, her eyes landing on her brother standing in the doorway, as if her very thoughts had summoned him. His brown eyes sparkled.

"Ye are home!" She looped her arm around his broad shoulders, pulling him close despite his travel-stained tunic and cloak. "How was the journey? Did ye all survive?"

"Good and yes," Hunter said, choosing to answer her questions in one breath. "We're all safe and ready for the ceremony. I think this year we've all proved our worth. I left a few snowy rabbits from the mountains on our doorstep as my contribution to the feast, and Amlo brought back a whole bear. He does his family proud."

"*Ye* do me proud." Serena stood back, a smile playing at her lips. Hunter's voice had deepened from what she last remembered, and his hair now reached beyond his ears, giving off the look of a rough warrior.

He talked as she prepared the rabbits, telling her about his journey south, of living in the wilderness high in the mountains with only his dagger. "I don't know what became of the lads, because it was just me," he told her excitedly as the meat cooked. "I met several mountain men who told me tales and gave me food. Then I hiked to the top of a ridge and made camp, staying there the rest of the month."

Hunter's voice soothed Serena as she completed her share of the feast each woman in the village would have a hand in preparing. She rebraided her dark brown hair, the beat of the drums already echoing through the cottage. Outside, the elders called the folk to the community lodge for the Ceremony.

"Ye know... I thought about Da and Mam while I was up there," Hunter said as she tied a leather thong around her thick braid. "About when we lived in the south and were like all the other folk."

"And spoke like all the other folk," Serena finished, pulling a shawl around her shoulders.

"Aye, but then I thought about here in the north, I can prove myself, while down south we were judged for..." His voice drifted off, but Serena knew. Her and Mam's Marks had been everything in the south, a death-wish waiting to happen.

Here, she kept her secret hidden, and Hunter stood a chance.

"And up there I just knew we were where we need to be, here near the capitol," Hunter continued. "Here I can help the folk if I become a soldier."

Serena nodded, her throat constricting with emotion. "But promise me ye will stay safe? Promise that when ye are making that difference in the world, ye won't forget who ye are and all that Da and Mam taught us?

"Aye, but only if ye promise me that ye won't go using your Gift?"

"Mayhap..." She allowed little sparks to dash through her fingers, filling the air around them with playful flames. "But Gifts weren't meant to be hidden...Because ye never know when I may get a strong urge to burn something...or someone."

Hunter laughed. "Fine then. But if ye get yeself killed because of it, then I'm going to come and ye will have me to contend with."

Serena closed her hand, the sparks vanishing. "Deal." She reached up on the shelf above her cot and brought down her knife that she used to cut Hunter's hair. Holding the blade in her left hand, she ran her fingers through his tangled strands, trimming them away from his eyes.

"And when I'm gone and a man, will ye take care of Wolfe for me?"

"Ye have my word that the mutt will never be far from me." She paused. "I wish... I wish things were different, but I'm proud of ye, Hunter." Stepping back, she brushed the dirt away from his cheek with the pad of her thumb, then smoothed his unruly hair from his eyes. "*Now* ye are ready."

Serena held back the bearskin rug that hung from the door, and together brother and sister stepped out into the cool dusk. Air clear as a mountain stream rushed through her lungs and emotion threatened to spill over her eyes. Every fiber of her being dreaded this moment, their last night in the same village.

Once the soldiers came to take away the lads, she may never see him again. The folk didn't know what happened to their sons and brothers who were taken from them. The rumors said they were brainwashed, put under a spell to go against the Sindaleerians and hold allegiance only to the king.

Serena shivered. May that never become true for Hunter.

The beat of the drums continued to echo through the now-quiet village as the folk gathered in the lodge, already enjoying the festivities.

Stars began to appear in the heavens, hovering over the Northern Mountains as the last rays of sunshine disappeared behind the dark veil of night. Thatched cottages remained dark, candles extinguished. Serena ducked into the lodge behind Hunter, the beat of the drums vibrating under her bare feet.

The air filled with the laughter of children and the chant of the elders. Old folk sat in the back watching the fray, as the young men and women danced at the center of the room. Excitement hung in the air, the fires cooking good food to be shared.

The village Head Elder, Calder, his white hair

flowing like snow down his back, stepped forward into the circle of lads and lasses and raised his hands, demanding a hush to fall over the crowd. The noise ceased in an instant.

"Lads of Sindaleer," Calder began. "You have been chosen to take part in the Ceremony of the Elect. Your folk are happy to see you lads begin manhood as Destiny allows." Then he proceeded to speak of the Ceremony and its rules, as though the lads and rest of the folk had not heard it all once a year for their entire lives.

"You've been out alone in separate parts of the wilderness, hunting and living as men with only your dagger. For thirty days we have awaited your return—and the ceremony deeming our lads of ten and five summers now *men*."

Hunter's face glowed with pride as he listened to the Elder speak. Her brother had dreamed of this day for as long as she could remember, where he would show his worth as a man and his wooden sword would be replaced with one of steel.

"Now, lads, step forth with your contribution to this celebration."

Hunter took a step near the center of the crowd, holding the basket of meat up with one hand. "For this feast I give ye the snowy rabbits from high in the southern mountains." A murmur of appreciation sounded through the lodge.

Another lad joined Hunter. A red scar rested across his nose and mouth, giving him the look of a warrior fresh from battle. "I contribute the venison from the deer I killed on the plains near the country of

Minogloria."

And soon the other five lads of ten and five summers joined Hunter and the scarred warrior, bringing their meat, and proudly proving that they had succeeded in surviving alone. Serena watched Calder as he listened to the lads' accounts, pleasure softening his face.

This year all the lads in the ceremony had found success.

"You have proved your worth as men in the eyes of the folk—do you not all agree with me, village of Aedre?"

The folk cheered, and the beat of the drums echoed as the drummers caught onto the excitement.

"Then let us begin the Ceremony—" Calder paused, his words cut short as a horn echoed outside, ringing off the hills. Serena's heart caught in her throat, her eyes meeting Hunter's. The villagers' murmurs circled the lodge.

"'Tis not good," a wrinkled lady beside Serena muttered. "That is a horn from Bron."

The mutts began barking. A pounding of hooves resounded outside the lodge, and Calder pushed through the folk, the other elders and menfolk joining him. Calder disappeared outside. A hush blanketed the tent.

A visit from the king's men only meant trouble. Serena swallowed, glancing down at her wrists covered by the folds of her sleeve.

"What is the meaning of this?" Calder's voice echoed in the still. "You interrupted our Ceremony, soldier."

"Only to do the king's work," came the gruff

reply. "Bring your lads out here. The party's over."

2

A man stepped into the doorway of the lodge, his black hair cut short against his head in the soldier's fashion, a sword strapped to his side. His dark eyes swept over the large group, falling on the lads from the ceremony. "Folk of Sindaleer!" he called. "I have been ordered by King Thayer to find all lads no younger than thirteen years, to train them to be soldiers for king and country. I now ask that you all step outdoors."

Serena glanced at Hunter, his mouth set in a hard line. The folk pressed around her, their talk drowning out all thought. Hunter joined her. "What's going to happen to the village?" he whispered low into her ear, as the flow shoved them towards the door. "There'll be no sons to help the widows."

Serena's heart beat like war drums in her ears, the excitement once hanging in the air gone like the mist of morning. What *would* happen to the widows without their sons to help them with the harvest? How would they survive if they did not have their lads to bring in meat as the cold set in?

Standing in the back of the crowd of villagers as they swarmed outdoors, she had to crane her neck to see above the many heads. Blinding darkness hung over the land as soldiers now circled the confused folk. Many of the men were dressed in tunics and trousers. Flaming torches illuminating their sullen faces and the spears and circular shields in their hands.

"What business does the king have with these lads?" a man called out, his hand firmly on his son's shoulder. "He's enough of his own men! Besides, young rider, my son is only three and ten, a mite young to be a soldier in my eyes. That age, he's just old enough to clean off the battlefield."

Murmurs of agreement from others followed, but the soldier ignored them.

"The lads will be under the service of our Lord Thayer for only five years before being able to return to their homes."

"Five years!" A grandfather with only his young grandson spat at the rider. "I'll be dead before I see my lad go with the likes of you and your king."

The rider, however, disregarded the villager, as he had the others, with the wave of his hand. "No matter. If they do not come, then I am ordered to burn down this village and all others who refuse."

Hunter grew pale. Serena could feel her own face turn white with fear. A shiver slipped over her, her hands

19

slick with sweat despite the cold.

When none of the lads stepped forwards, the leader of the soldiers motioned for his men to dismount. "Begin to burn the bloody place down if they continue to refuse."

"Wait!"

Serena's heart dropped at the voice.

Everyone turned as Hunter stepped up to the front, tossing the bone dagger from his belt to the ground. "We'll go peacefully. Hurt no one and burn nothing." Glancing back at her, he thumped a fist against his chest. *I. Will. Return.*

Her and Hunter's secret promise. The one Da made to her each time he left on a long hunting trip, each time Mam kissed her goodnight when she was a small lass, too afraid to sleep.

As one by one the young lads took their place by the leader, Serena's heart burned with fury and fear. Her gaze collided with Hunter's, and despite the darkness, she saw that his hands trembled.

The voices of the villagers continued around Serena, some in protest, others in defeat. And then all but two lads remained, and she recognized them as the sons of two widows.

"Let me at least stay with my Mam until after the harvest," Bow, the first lad, pleaded. "It is only yet the beginning of fall, and she has no one else."

A murmur of protest against the king rose up in defense of Bow's words, and the leader faltered, glancing from his men to Bow. "King Thayer has his orders, lad."

Nay. Serena's heart sank in her chest. Bow's

crippled mam would have next to nothing now, left to fend for herself. She glanced from Bow to the man on his high horse, fear and anger mingling together.

"How can ye be so heartless?" She hadn't realized she'd said this aloud until the man turned her way, his black eyes piercing hers, void of emotion.

"I have my orders." He nodded towards the soldiers and the lads. "Move out."

"Nay, please!" Serena rushed forward, swallowing the bile rising in her throat. "Can't ye show some mercy on two poor widows? Surely ye can spare these two lads."

The man turned back towards her, his gaze holding hers. "What do you think you're doing?"

"I beg of ye, my Lord. Have a heart and spare these two lads for their Mams' sakes."

In that moment, she would have sworn to the gods that he'd faltered, that mayhap she had won. But then— "I still say I have to follow orders." He nodded to the soldier riding beside him. "Kene, lock her in a cell for the night—the maiden doesn't know who she's talking to."

3

Serena shivered, blinking in the dusk. Light trickled through a barred window above her, illuminating the place where she sat. Behind her, more bars met her gaze.

Pain pulsed through her neck and head. Cold seeped through the floor and walls. The night had gone on like a never-ending nightmare, and she wished with every breath she drew that it had been nothing more than one of those tales of doom Hunter liked so well. Except in those stories, the captives always found freedom, the folk stood up for justice, and the evil king would have never remained on the throne.

The soldiers had brought her to a jail cell, and she now sat in the castle dungeon underneath the capital city of Bron. Hunter had walked at the head of the group the night before, his shoulders back, tall and proud. And as her captor had paused at the castle, Hunter had turned. "I

22

love you," he'd mouthed.

And then he was gone.

Serena's heart tripped as she continued to gaze through the bars holding her captive. Rows of cells continued down the dark corridor, all empty. Cold silence met her ears.

She was alone.

Serena crumpled to the ground and rubbed her pounding temples. Her head swam, so she closed her eyes, resting her forehead against the ice-cold wall.

The stench of death surrounded her, taunting her, reminding her of the lives lost. When King Thayer had waged war on Sindaleer over ten years hence and taken the throne, he'd sent the former king's soldiers, advisors, the Elders of all villages, and any important men down to the castle dungeon, giving them no food or water. He'd wished to show the folk that anyone who dared rise up against him would be punished.

Severely.

And now she sat where they'd spent their last moments all those years ago.

The sound of boots alerted her of another's presence, and two men turned the corner, one leading the other into the cell beside hers. Peering into the dim light, she recognized the dark-haired soldier who had come to her village, but now a red gash stood out on one of his clean-shaven cheeks. Blood dripped down his chin, staining his leather jerkin and white tunic.

He swiped the crimson stream away with the back of his hand, his brooding gaze meeting hers. His olive-toned skin was far tanner than that of a

Sindaleerian, and his glare felt like a slap.

The cell door shut, locking him inside the bare room beside her, only a wall of bars to separate them. The footsteps of his captor echoed as he pounded back up the stairs to the second floor. A stiff quiet descended.

He kicked the door, muttering curses under his breath. Now in the light of morning, he looked to be no more than twenty summers, if that. His pushed back sleeves revealed a snake tattoo that curled around his wrist, the head reared back as if to strike.

Then the man's eyes turned back in her direction, sliding up and down her frame as if she sat on display. Recognition dawned. "Ah, the lass from the village."

"Aye, and ye should be ashamed. Ye have taken good lads away from many needy families."

"I'm a soldier, and I have to take orders."

"Young lads are not soldiers, my Lord. They are only warriors in training."

Her fellow prisoner raised his eyebrows. "Ah, but you know nothing of who I am or any matters of the king. Mayhap, you were taught to kill off the wounded at the end of battle, but I am sure the tactics of Thayer are far above you."

"Be that as it may, ye act like nothing more than a puppet for the king." Serena's face grew hot under the man's intense gaze. Embarrassed about her sudden outburst, she turned her back to him.

"Perhaps it seems that way," came the reply behind her. "But let's not judge one another. Men trained as soldiers are in the past; our king wants lads who can be molded and shaped."

Enough. Serena whirled around. "*I* was locked up for no reason. I'm sure this is not your case."

The man's eyebrows rose. Amusement fled his eyes, replaced with an almost terrifying hatred. "I am Milosh." The name slipped from his mouth like poison.

Serena's heart skipped a beat from cold shock. She'd just been arguing with the king's own son.

✗

When the maiden heard his name, her face blanched as if she would be sick, and she turned away. Mayhap she thought he would have her executed for talking so, and Milosh bloody well hoped that he hid his amusement from this peasant lass who so easily defied him, taking him down at every remark. He found her expression almost comical.

He slid back down the stone wall that felt like ice through his leather jerkin. He could hear the lass in the cell beside him, pacing back and forth. Water dripped from somewhere above him.

Milosh closed his eyes. The quiet soothed his frayed nerves; the anger and darkness that usually held his heart captive, for a time, fleeing.

He felt more peace sitting in a cell where no one expected anything of him, than back in the castle. Here, the demons tearing at his sanity felt miles away. Here, he was alone.

The lass sneezed.

Well, except for the maiden.

Time slid by, and his eyes grew heavy with

25

fatigue. At first he had thought nothing of the assignment his father had bestowed upon him. It had been nothing but a command from the king that he carried out to simply keep the peace.

But, after the deed had been completed, his conscience had argued with him.

He'd wished to do nothing that would risk the throne. He never wanted to give up that place that would one day fall into his possession. However, the faces of those young lads had burned in his mind as he'd rode back from the village.

And bloody hell, the maiden he had locked up was right.

"If I am supposed to follow such commands as taking young lads away from their folk where they're needed, then I will see my father," he growled at King Thayer's advisor. "That or I will leave and never return." He drew in an earth-shattering breath. "Where is he?"

"He's in the throne room speaking with some men. He wishes to not be disturbed."

Milosh eyed the doors leading into the throne room and back at Selwyn. "I care not." He threw open the door, the bang echoing in the hall.

Thayer, king of Sindaleer, the man who had assaulted his mother and taken the throne from the rightful king twenty years ago, glanced up from where he was sitting.

That face—the mirror of his own—was the reason he could never look himself in the eye, for he loathed seeing his hated father's visage staring back at him. The dark hair, the almost-black eyes, all of it had come from him.

Thayer looked from Milosh to Selwyn. "What is the meaning of this?"

"I refuse to leave until you explain why I am forced to take lads from their homes when they are needed to help their folk."

Thayer waved his hand to Milosh as he continued to study the papers strewn out on the long table. "Get him out of here."

"Nay! Show some face, you coward!" But the guards were already carrying him out.

The doors to the throne room slammed, silencing his screams.

Milosh's eyes flew open, his heart threatening to shatter the bones in his chest. The silence roared in his ears as the water continued to drip from the ceiling and slide down his face.

He could feel fellow prisoner's intent gaze, her expression hidden by the dusk of evening. Their eyes collided, before Milosh turned away, not wanting her to see the pain.

4

"*Once upon a time the god of mischief walked the earth and decided to steal fire from the folk. He slipped down late one night, and took all ability to create fire. The folk woke the next day and the women stirred the coals, but try as they might, they couldn't create a spark.*

They lost all means to cook or warm their little ones, and they cried out in despair. 'We'll all die,' they said. 'Fire is light and life and now we shall surely perish.'

But one boy, Elior, laughed and said that despair had made weaklings of his people. He took up his bow and—"

"*Serena!*"

Serena stopped her story at Mum's harsh voice. Her mother stood over her, her lips pressed into a hard line.

"*Come help me, daughter.*"

Serena's young audience scampered off, and

Serena hung her head, following Mum to the cottage. She slipped under the animal skin doorway, Mam's fingers closing around her arm.

> *"The Tale of Elior, eh?" she said softly.*
> *"Aye," Serena whispered.*
> *"The tale of the only one who stood."*
> *Serena gazed down at her bare feet.*
> *Mam's gentle hand reached down, titling Serena's*

face so their eyes met. "The tale of rebellion, aye? Serena, the king has forbidden stories that teach such things. If the soldiers heard ye speak, ye'd be taken from me." She leaned down, placing a soft kiss on Serena's forehead. "My daughter of quiet fire. How I wish I could give ye the freedom ye crave."

✘

For one night, Serena sat in the damp cell, curled up in a ball, hugging her knees to her chest to fight the cold, hoping beyond hope that she would be free by morning.

Relief spilled over her as the sun finally dawned, allowing beautiful light into her cell, the sight contradicting the smells of human waste and death that overpowered all other senses. Serena's head swam with relief when she heard the jingle of keys; her legs, numb from the cold, almost gave way beneath her. She licked her cracked lips, tasting blood and grime.

A towering soldier opened the door to the cell and ushered her out with a gloved hand. As she exited the Destiny-forsaken place, Serena couldn't help but glance over her shoulder. Milosh still sat on the floor of his own locked room, his eyes closed, his head resting on the wall. The hard lines on his forehead made him appear foreboding even in sleep.

"Go on upstairs and return home," the soldier told her roughly. "You are released."

Serena tugged her thumbs into the loopholes at the edge of her dresses' sleeves to make sure her Marks weren't visible. Glancing over her shoulder one last time, she saw Milosh's eyes were opened, but his gaze stared beyond her.

Taking the steps slowly, she leaned against the wall for support. She dared not look down as she climbed, for fear her head would betray her. Serena longed for nothing more than a drink of water and a slice of bread dipped in deer gravy like her Mam always made during the fall season.

At last she made it to the top, her bare feet slipping once or twice on the last few stairs in a liquid she didn't want to consider. Below her stood the dark abyss, and she shuddered, vowing to never again set herself in a position where she'd be forced to return.

Turning away from the dungeon, she made her way down the hall, beyond the kitchens, and to the servant's door. What would she do now? With Hunter gone, returning to the cottage was now the last thing she wanted to do. "Serena!"

She stopped and turned to find Clovis, a serving lass and girl from her village, chasing her down the hall from the kitchens. "What is it, Clovis?"

Clovis held out an apple. "What happened? Are you free to go?"

Serena nodded, taking the apple and biting through the wrinkled skin. She and Clovis had never been close, but Clovis always took the time to say a good morning to her each day.

"It's only because your family wasn't like the rest." Clovis lowered her voice, glancing behind Serena at the soldier guarding the servant's entrance. "A lot of us do what we're told without a word, but your Da and brother would say and do things that let folk know you're against the king..."

Serena knew they were different—more than Clovis could guess. "I have to go. Thank ye for the apple."

After turning toward the door, she gave a weak nod to the guard and hurried through the dew-soaked grass. The morning sun hung beyond the mountains, turning the new leaves orange in its rays. She ran all the way to the cottage, crept inside and leaned against the wall, breathing hard.

Her body shook from the cold and fatigue. She drew some water from the bucket, hands shaking as she took a drink. The water burned as the icy liquid ran down her parched throat.

Wolfe brushed against her leg. "Oh, ye had someone untie ye, did ye, lad?" Serena brushed a hand over his thick white fur and leaned against the table, trying to steady her racing heart.

She could hear a rooster crowing and children laughing outside her cottage. Ignoring the tremor in her hands, she reached for the hard bread that Hunter had left on the little table the day before. She took a bite, letting the hard crumbs dissolve in her mouth.

She didn't want to think about the fact that for five years their paths wouldn't cross unless by chance. He would come back, twenty summers, a full-grown man with a beard the color of his red hair.

Changed forever.

Serena swallowed the rest of the bread, the lump in her throat growing. Her stomach could no longer handle the food. She wished she'd agreed when Hunter had begged her to flee to Minogloria with him two summers past, a country where folk with marks and ink green tattoos were all treated equally.

But fear had held her back.

As it always had. She lived in a world where you were taught to fear, taught to fear those stronger, to fear authority and bow no matter the cost.

She soaked in the memories of this place, at the patch of bare floor where Hunter had once slept by her side, the place where stories were all they had to get through the long nights without Mam and Da.

Hot tears burned the back of her eyes, but she refused to give in to them. This was no time to be weak, but to remind herself that she could only blame herself.

Mayhap if she'd said yes to Hunter then none of this would've ever happened.

A shade of darkness fell over the land, and night came. The moon hid behind a veil of luminous clouds, enclosing a shadow that crept along the wall circling the castle.

Slowly the figure of Enid, Gifted and one of the Marked, darted closer until it stood but a breath from the servant's door leading through the wall and into the inner courtyard. A slender hand slid out from behind a crimson cloak and pushed.

Locked.

Enid gazed around. Pressing her back against the wall, she reached for the dagger at her side, but met only air. She had forgotten the dagger.

Again.

A breath passed by, and she remained still, meshing with the darkness until she and the wall appeared from afar as one. A wolf howled and mutts barked down in the village of Aedre.

She heard footsteps coming through the courtyard on the other side of the wall. Cursing, she closed her eyes, drawing in a steady breath. She would make do. Weapons were needed but not wanted. Not with her, not when she had gifts more powerful than that of a dagger.

As a serving lass stepped through the doorway, Enid dove forward. She reached out a hand, dragging the lass to the ground. The girl let out a shriek, staring up at her captor with wide eyes.

Enid locked eyes with the lass. The girl tried to stand but suddenly dropped to the ground, moaning and grabbing her head. She opened her mouth as if to scream, but pain silenced her. Her eyes closed as the darkness consumed her.

Enid grimaced as she stepped over the lifeless

form. Violence towards innocents was not her way, but in times such as these, extreme measures must be taken.

She slipped through the door, shutting the barrier and shoving the bar back over the wooden panel. She drew the hood of her cloak away from her head, her dark hair falling over her face. Throwing back her shoulders, she walked with purpose through the darkened courtyard and up to the servants' entrance.

This door opened with no hesitation.

Victory.

She stepped inside, her cloak blending in with the blackened castle. Burning torches flickered on the walls, and she took one. Light splattered across walls and doors.

"Where, where?" she murmured.

Not an ounce of fear claimed her, only satisfaction that she'd come this far. Voices and the bangs of pots and pans from the kitchen met her ears, and a smile played at her mouth. Maids spoke with loose tongues, and she'd once heard while in a village last fall that the prince's chambers were only a flight of stairs away from the kitchen.

Enid hurried down the hall, pressing her back against the stone, listening to the kitchen maid's mindless chatter. They spoke in low undertones, their laughter filtering through the doorway as she took her chance. Hurrying past the kitchen door, her breath quickened with excitement.

Turning into a stairwell, she took the steps two at a time, her cloak flying out behind her. Nearing the top, she flung open another door into an additional corridor, the flaming torches mounted on the walls illuminating the hall.

And the lone door at the far end.

Her lips thinned into a hard line as she crossed the short corridor. She pauses, preparing her mind. The words of a foreign tongue slid from her mouth, the chant rising. Her torch sputtered, threatening to die.

She stopped, drawing in a sharp breath. Her hand reached for the knob, her tattooed Marks peeking out from under her sleeves. She opened the door, and set her torch down on the floor against the stone wall.

From the low flicker of the torch behind her, she could see a cot to her right. The prince should be sleeping, unaware of her presence. And when he awoke from the pain it would be of little consequence. He would die no matter what ... and she couldn't help but anticipate the look in his eyes as she tore the life from him.

Enid took two small steps toward the cot. She needed his eyes, but his head was buried deep beneath the furs.

A warning bell clung. The sound mingled with the cry of the drums beating to their heavy rhythm in the courtyard. Her muscles tightened, and she muttered an angry oath.

The lady cast her gaze over her shoulder. She could hear the pounding of steps through the castle, the shouts of angry guards.

At any moment, Milosh would wake and overpower her. She had no choice.

"Your doom is before you. Rise, Milosh, son of Thayer."

Milosh opened his eyes, and his gaze locked with

35

hers. A breath passed between them, the air growing still as he reached for his sword. "Who are you?"

Enid laughed and looked deep into his eyes, still hazy from sleep. She concentrated, poured every ounce of strength into his confused gaze.

Milosh screamed and grabbed his head. The sword clattered to the ground. He tumbled from the cot, unable to pull his head away from her, held captive by an invisible force.

Milosh, son of Thayer, was about to greet death.

Footsteps pounded their way up the stairs. They would soon be upon her.

With a cry of frustration, she broke the spell on the writhing prince. Whirling around, Enid ran back whence she'd come, leaving Milosh half-conscious on the floor. She wished her magic had grown stronger so she might cast a shadow over his most recent thoughts and he would forget her.

She had risked everything to come here, but she didn't care. Milosh had tasted her wrath and he *would* taste it again.

Enid stopped at the stairs entrance and waited for the guards to arrive. Two ran up and both met with her gaze of agony. Then she fled down the stairs. After glancing around and seeing nothing but darkness, she ran down the courtyard. She escaped into the shadows, fleeing through the gate and into the quiet city of Bron where her horse stood tied by the market plaza.

She swung up onto her mare, her head swimming as she kicked the creature into a gallop. King Thayer would do best to heed her warning—his son was not safe.

Darkness enveloped her, warning horns beginning to echo through the city.

As the wind roared around her, her memory began to fade, abandoning her as it most always did, for only a time—the one curse to this Gift. Glancing over her shoulder, she bit back a vile oath. "I will remember again. And soon I will be back."

5

Serena pushed her sleeves over her Marks, empty water pail in hand as she walked down the path to the stream. Two small lasses with their brown hair braided in tiny cornrows, ran by her, playing catch-me.

"Hello," Serena called.

The two lasses gazed up at her, their eyes sparkling in the morning light. "Hello, Serena," they answered in unison. "Can we play with Wolfe?"

Serena nodded, and together the children and mutt ran off, Wolfe barking at their heels. Serena smiled at the bittersweet sight. She remembered she and Hunter playing with the village dogs in similar fashion. Life had been simpler back then, a taste of freedom she did not have now.

She continued through the village, leaving the small lasses and Wolfe behind as they ran through the dew-covered fields. Smoke curled up from thatched cottages, and an elderly blind woman called out greetings as her footsteps drew near. "Is that ye, Serena?"

"Aye, Sun. 'Tis me." Serena clasped the wrinkled hand. "How are ye this morn'?"

"Fine and dandy. Yeself?"

"Just fine." Seren stared into the cloudy eyes that looked unseeing into her own. Sun lived alone, and Serena often visited her during long winter evenings. With Sun, she could be herself.

She could both use her Gift and remain unafraid in her elderly friend's company. Also, Sun was not like the other villagers. Because of her lost sight, she depended on Serena, needed her.

Such a sad truth. That those blind could see the most.

Serena bade her neighbor farewell, and continued through the village towards the stream. The sun, hidden by milky clouds, fought the dark clouds to shine. A group of young lads argued as they played with wooden swords.

She continued down the path, nodding to villagers who made their way back from the stream. Up ahead she heard an elder and his wife speaking together, their voices carrying through the sight of the wind.

"The prince was said to have gone mad for several hours," the elder was saying. "The lady was one of the Gifted, if the rumors are true."

Serena stopped, her mouth dry. The couple stood only yards away, hidden by thick brush and trees.

"Gifteds became rare," his wife muttered. "What's making them brave now?"

Instinctively, Serena's hand moved to her covered wrists, the hand clenching her water bucket going white.

"Did they find her, the lady who did it?" The elder's wife dropped her voice, Serena nearly unable to catch her words.

"Nay, they say—" And the words of the elder became lost altogether as they continued towards the stream.

Serena remained hidden in the brush, her mind spinning. Who was this Marked lady seeking to murder the prince? She sucked in a breath of air. Her hands shook.

She hated this, hated other Gifteds causing fear and shame. They only made life harder for folk like her. They were the reason she had to keep her Gift a secret.

After the purge twenty years hence, where Gifteds were branded and those caught using their Gifts were beheaded, Serena's kind appeared to have all but disappeared.

Some flew to neighboring countries or the mountains in the south, further away from King Thayer's spies. Others perished, outcasts in the land.

Serena turned back up the path, refusing to go down to the stream and have to talk with the elder and his wife about the Gifted in the castle. *You have nothing to fear, Serena. Go back to the village. All is well. Gossip. 'Tis all gossip.*

Rumors and truth often mixed, causing villages to question the validity of what came in and out of the castle. Folk loved a good story, and truth could become twisted quicker than she could light a fire.

Serena continued whence she'd come, her back to the busybodies. Dawn brushed the sky with its warm rays, lighting her home and the capital of Bron beyond. This morning, the chill had convinced her to slip on her leather moccasins and heavy woolen dress. The red leaves of autumn crunched under her feet, and the corn in the fields stood tall, ready for harvesting.

Summer was gone and with it, so much more.

Serena gazed up at the tall apple tree sheltering the path. Dropping the bucket, she grabbed a hold of the lowest branch and pulled herself up. Wolfe lay at the base of the tree, his head between his paws.

Soon folk from the village would be headed out to the animals in the fields or the orchards, but for many, breakfast sat on the table. In the past Serena never worked in the orchards this early. She would feed Hunter and do the wash, before heading to the city to trade and buy wares.

Serena balanced on the branch as she leaned against the trunk, resting her head back on a branch. Sunlight filtered through the trees of the orchard. Mist danced over the fields, surrounding the men beginning to wander out to begin their labor. A bird landed above her head, singing softly.

Despite the beauty and quiet of this work, Serena's heart ached for Hunter, and for them to be children once more. She ached for home and simplicity and childlike innocence.

Now gone like the mist in the fields once the light of the sun touched down.

The hairs on the back of Serena's neck bristled.

Her eyes scanned the surrounding trees, and down below her, Wolfe pricked up his ears. The bird above Serena's head ceased its song.

She pushed back the feeling of watchful eyes only paces away. Her fingertips glowed. Standing on her perch, the tree gave her no view but the ground below.

Serena glanced down at Wolfe.

Gone.

Her heart beat fiercely. She drew in another breath. Now was not the time for one of her attacks.

Breathe. Breathe. Breathe.

She coaxed herself to stay the panic. Her head swam and black dots formed in her vision. All she could feel was the wind, the bitter wind as it taunted her terror. Grabbing a low-hanging branch, she swung down from the tree, her fear of falling growing stronger than the fear of the unknown.

As her feet touched wet grass, she instantly turned a full circle, ready to convince herself that her imagination had created another false story.

"Do not move."

Cold metal pressed against the back of her neck, and a hand smothered her from speaking. "Do not move," the voice repeated. The voice of a lady. Warm air, the breath from someone's lungs, tickled her ear.

Serena shivered. "What do ye want?" Her lungs constricted, the words coming out in short gasps.

"Say nothing." The dagger pricked deeper.

Serena didn't dare to swallow.

Her captor shoved her down to her knees. "If you promise to stay your legs from running away, then I will stay my hand from slitting your throat." The knife withdrew. "Do you agree?"

Serena tried to nod.

The hands left her throat and mouth, and the lady stepped from around Serena, her dark eyes flicking to Serena's wrists.

"Are you Serena, peasant and sister of Hunter?"

"What about her?"

"I have a message that she may find of some interest." The lady leaned closer, and Serena could smell lavender on her skin and fur dress. She wore a crimson cape like dark blood, the hood casting a shadow over her face. "I am Enid, sorceress and bearer of the same Marks as you."

"I'm not Serena." She took in a deep breath, willing warmth to flood her body, to flood her fingertips with liquid fire.

Enid laughed. She leaned closer, her eyes flashing mockingly. "Ah, but my eyes see all. You cannot lie to me. I have watched you for many days. I know who you are." She paused. "You too have felt the effects of King Thayer's reign. You know what has happened to our kind, do you not?"

Serena nodded, keeping her gaze level with Enid. *Remain calm. Let her see nothing.* "We live in fear each day, do we not?"

Again Serena nodded. She knew that her hands were glowing now, smoke circling around her fingertips.

"Then, we must act if no folk will, must we not?" Enid continued. "Surely you see King Thayer is planning evil on our country, that after over two decades of his reign, still we are oppressed? And do you know, Serena of Aedre, that after him, his son, who he has trained, will take the throne? You know this, do you not?"

Another nod. *Now!* Without taking her eyes off the lady, she jumped to her feet and lifted her hands. *Liquid fire, flow.*

Enid screamed a curse and dodged the fireball Serena flung at her. But it was the expression of both excitement and fear that shook Serena's courage.

Pain exploded inside her mind. Every tangible thought and action fled except making it stop.

Pain.

Pain.

Only pain.

Serena cried out, falling back to her knees. She grabbed her head, rocking back and forth. White lights flashed behind her closed eyelids. She was going to die.

And just as suddenly as the torture started, it vanished. Serena felt her head being yanked back. "Open your eyes," Enid demanded.

Serena obeyed, tears blurring her vision. Heat poured from Enid's fury. "I hoped we could avoid pain," she said tightly. "But apparently that is impossible." She tugged harder at Serena's hair, making her cry out. "You should understand that we are one and the same, outcasts and feared because of a king who doesn't belong on the throne. My request is simple: kill the prince, and if you do not—know this—then your brother will die at my hand, I will be sure of that."

Serena's stomach threatened to spew its contents on the ground. The throbbing in her head felt like a dull ache. Her throat closed in fear. The prince's dark face shot into her mind, his emotionless eyes as he scowled at her from his cell in the castle.

"I have no way to get to the prince," Serena whispered.

"You haven't heard the prophecy." Enid let go of her. "I suppose that is not surprising considering the words of the Seer were before your time." She uttered a low laugh. "If you really are Serena, wielder of fire and from the village of Aedre—and from what just happened, there is no point in denying it—I know you will find a way."

Enid straightened, her long fingers reaching to pull her cloak's hood back over her head. "Understand me, Serena, that I only want to do what is right, that I only wish for light in this blackened land. Measures must be taken in days of war. You don't realize the potential you have if this prophecy speaks true. You alone may hold the power to restore Sindaleer."

Serena swallowed, her mouth gritty. Leaves rustled in the wind. No voices from the fields met her ears. Serena and Enid were alone.

They stared, one at the other, neither moving.

"Realize this," Enid said calmly. "I mean what I say." She began to walk away, carrying with her the sharp flower scent. "I will return. Be ready. The time for King Thayer and Milosh's doom is soon upon them." Enid disappeared towards the Northern Mountains, away from the village of Aedre, but not gone forever.

A heavy white moon hung in the starlit sky. Dense fog covered the land like a heavy blanket, drifting low over the fields and villages below the Northern Mountains.

Hunter glanced over his shoulder, stopping to catch his breath. Cold air wrapped around him. He cocked his head, listened, and then plodded on through the dense forest.

Every nerve in his body hummed. He'd done it. He'd made it out of the castle of Bron, and as much as he could tell, he wasn't being followed.

Only half a mile further, and he'd arrive at his destination. Hunter had spent the last few days preparing for this moment, the first time since arriving in Bron that he would escape the castle, alone.

Milosh, his eyes heavy from the mead Hunter had poured him, had retired early, and Hunter had feigned going back to the barracks to sleep. Instead, he'd slipped through the servants' back gate, praying the gods would be on his side tonight.

If he was caught, death would be his.

At last the cave rose up in sight, a giant shadowy mass in the dusk, hidden by fallen trees and heavy brush. The sharp scent of the woodsmoke drifted into the night. Hunter ducked under the low doorway and tossed his bow and quiver at the opening.

Bringing weapons into any Sindaleerian meeting was a sign of disrespect and mistrust.

Ten other caped figures gathered around the warmth of the fire in the middle of the dim room, and he joined them, sitting against the far wall by his friend

Destin. A little lad sat away from the others, a messenger for the group, and the smallest in their band.

The leader, Fell, stepped into the room from where Hunter had entered, his long hair tied back with a leather thong. "I thank you all for coming," he said. He took the time to hold the gaze of them as he set his shield by the door. "I didn't know if some of you would make it."

One of the older men of the group, who had reached fifty winters, lit his pipe. "What news do ya bring us, Fell?"

Fell sat down with the ring of men, lighting his own pipe and taking a long drawl. "The Ceremony of the Elect has begun across Sindaleer, and you young lot missed it. Thayer took ya before your time."

"It's high time we make further plans to get our lads out of this mess," the eldest of the smugglers pointed out. "Not just the ones near us, but the ones further down towards the border where news of King Thayer snatching our lads will come too late. They won't have time to flee, and will be taken unawares. I don't care if the fiendish king does hear about us—it's about time he did know some of the men folk are going against him."

"It is not as simple as you say," Destin interjected. "I risked my neck coming out here tonight. This is Hunter's first time coming here since becoming a new addition to the king's ranks, and frankly I'm surprised he made it as quickly as he did."

"I almost didn't come," Hunter said. "But they've only just begun training, so we haven't been stuck with guard duty."

"Tell them you have a lass if they ask where you've been," another man said with jest.

Fell shook his head and raised his hands. "I thank ya for all risking your lives, but the men are right—we must do something. I've spoken with the Guardian leader, and they told us that they will take in any lads we can smuggle to them, train 'em proper to be Guardians instead of soldiers."

One of the lads, whom Hunter didn't know, stood up. "My Da says that Guardians are giving us folk a bad name to the King. If King Thayer sees us as lawbreakers, he'll become harder than he is now. I got a family to look after, and I can't have anything to do with the low-breaker Guardians, Fell."

Fell glanced around and raised his eyebrows. "Anyone else wish to leave?"

"Now hold up," the lad interjected. "I never said nothing about leaving."

"If you don't agree with us and our Guardian friends, we're going to ask ya to leave. We're a band of brothers, and I won't go and allow us to break away because of a disagreement."

The lad sat down, saying nothing. Hunter groaned inwardly, waiting for the worst.

The two older men at the meeting looked at each other, and one stood. "I don't like hearing talk about Guardians either. I can't put up with it anymore. They help us now and then, and I know a lot of the villagers are grateful, but I don't trust our lads going to them."

Hunter watched the man's companion. He held his eyes to the fire. One of the lads kicked him, and he sat upright again. "I've been thinking … I don't like this either, Fell. I agree that we should do something, but there's no one that I can really trust. Next year, when he turns eleven summers, I'm taking my lad to Minogloria myself." He shook his head firmly and got up, following his friend out the door, apology in his eyes.

Hunter's heart sank.

They couldn't give up now. For months they had plotted how to smuggle lads out of view of the king to be trained as warriors, and how to form an uprising in secret with the Guardians folk.

Nay, it would not all be in vain. Hunter turned to the three remaining new lads who were all under the age of twelve summers. "Well, are ye going to give up too? Just like that are we all goin' to give into the king who destroyed our lands? We've helped lads in the villages around us before, and we can't let the southerners be left on their own, can we now?"

Destin slapped him good naturedly on the back. "Thatta lad. Well, what do you three say? Will we defy the king, stealing lads from behind his back in the southern lands?"

The three in front of Destin and Hunter shifted where they sat, glancing at one another. Hunter knew that if one backed down, they all would.

He urged them with his eyes, pleading them to follow him and Destin. Bear, a lad Hunter's age, had made the pledge months before and also watched with silent eyes. He was one of the lads chosen to live with the Guardians in the secret paces of the mountains, training to rise against the King.

At last the tallest of the lads stood up and lifted his right hand over his heart in solemn vow. "I pledge my life to this cause. I place my life in the hands of Sindaleer, the country of which I am a son. If my life is taken because of it, then so be it."

The rest stood and did the same. Raising their hands, they waited for Destin and Hunter. Hunter stood tall and straight. "As a son of Sindaleer, I pledge my life to this cause." He looked at Fell. "My life I place so that I may help a cause much more vast than myself."

6

A long seven days drifted by for Serena. Every day she lived in fear, hoping that Destiny would allow her to wake up and find that the evil enchantress and her words had been some terrible dream.

Wolfe never left her side now; she made sure of that. The mutt slept on her legs at night, keeping her warm as the mornings frosted over with tiny ice crystals.

Serena would go through her chores around the cottage, and collect the food in exchange for supplies before curling up on the cot and sleeping. Some evenings she would slip into the back of the lodge and listen to the elders recount stories to the little lasses and lads.

She would close her eyes and pretend, for but a moment, to be one of them again.

Serena wished to see Hunter more than anything now, as the days shortened and the leaves on the trees began to fully change into red and gold. On the last morning of those long seven days, she knew she must talk with him, kiss his forehead, and ask how he fared.

She'd always been wary of soldiers, had been taught by her parents to beware of them and any folk associated with the king at all cost. They would only bring her pain and death.

But now she had no choice.

Serena rose early before the light spilled over the treetops, put on the remaining pair of moccasins she owned, and drank a little water from the bucket on the table. Her insides twisted too much to allow her to eat.

She called for Wolfe to join her, and he rose like an obedient servant from where he lay on her cot, following her out of the cottage and into the village. No one had risen yet, and darkness still shrouded the land as she made her away up the hill toward the castle.

The dusk swallowed her as she walked, the nighttime sounds beginning to die as a light glowed in the east. She remained alert, her body tense and ready for something out of the ordinary. A man continued his journey to the capitol Bron, traveling on the road less than half a mile away, only a brief silhouette in the dawn.

The dew of the tall grass clung to her dress, soaking through, the material clinging to her legs. Wolfe brushed up against her, his large body pressing against hers as they climbed the hill.

The only sounds now came from her footsteps, and peace warmed her heart despite the chill. If only life could remain this way: as beautiful as the land before sunrise. If only death wasn't the answer.

Serena eyed the curving road as she neared the

wall circling the castle, the cloaked man now out of sight. A twig snapped.

She stopped, begging her heartbeat to slow. Pausing on the damp hillside, she drew in more of the damp air. All around her, the land remained quiet.

Wolfe gazed up at her with his blue eyes, waiting for her to continue. He sensed nothing. Mayhap fear had addled her brain.

As the two of them reached the servant's gate in the castle wall, a sigh of relief escaped her lips. She turned the latch and slipped inside. Already the dark sky glowed with a tinge of pale pink in the east. She didn't have much time before the castle grounds would be bustling with soldiers preparing to train.

The servant's longhouse stood to her right behind the large stables. She edged along the walls around the castle. Her palm pressed against the stone, her cheeks warm from excitement and fear.

The smell of hay and dung from the barn several paces away mixed with the lingering odor of dirt and smoke drifting from the barracks. Wolfe whined in his throat as if he sensed Hunter was near, but Serena hushed him. Prince Milosh's bitter face formed in her mind but she shoved the image away, refusing to think she could see him here.

The barracks came into sight, the glow of the two torches mounted on the outside walls casting a faint light. Two longhouses crafted with logs from the Lowleen, and a thatched roof with smoke holes in the ceiling, made up the building where the men and lads slept and lived. Similar to the lodges used by the elders in the villages throughout Sindaleer, but also similar to the one she had lived in as a lass in the south.

Like home.

Her eyes scanning the castle grounds, she ran around the garrison, her hand moving along the wall. A small gasp escaped as her hand brushed up against something soft. She blinked in the shadows, her eyes adjusting to the dimness. An animal skin covered a doorway, blocking the inside from view.

Glancing down to make sure Wolfe still stood at her side, she pulled her sleeves over her wrists, hooking the loops near the cuff around her thumbs to hold the fabric in place.

She waited, her heart picking up speed. Inside she could hear the rough voices of men as they woke for the morning, no doubt smoking pipes and sharpening swords. Without taking any more time to consider what she was about to do, Serena stepped inside.

Smoke burned her eyes and nose. Serena glanced back as Wolfe sat down at the door, watching her with his blue eyes. And that's when her heart sank like a rock in her chest.

The room stood as silent as the pause before a thunderstorm.

She whirled around, dozens of faces meeting her gaze. Heat flamed her face.

Half of the soldiers smoked pipes of some heavy weed, the essence causing her throat to constrict. She coughed, covering her mouth with her sleeve.

Men of all ages sat around the long room, some drinking out of tall mugs, others once more beginning to sharpen their spears and swords as they waited for morning's light. In none of their faces did she see Hunter, yet her legs refused to move.

"What are you doing here?"

Serena stared up at a tall soldier with long hair that reached past his shoulders.

Someone whistled. "If you can't find who yer lookin' for pretty lady, I can take his place."

A few chuckled in agreement.

She froze. A hand reached out and touched her arm, and the fingers of fear curled around her.

"Serena?"

Serena whirled back around to find herself face to face with Hunter. His hair now cut in the short, soldier fashion he looked more like a warrior and less like the lad he would always be in her mind.

"What are ye doing here?" Hunter asked. "Ye are the most foolish sister!" His smile fell away, and concern lit his eyes. "What's wrong, Serena?"

"This your sister, Hunter?" One of the soldiers called out. "I wouldn't mind being introduced."

"I'm sure you wouldn't, Jervik," Hunter shot back.

Serena's heart resumed its normal beating. "Yes, I'm foolish perhaps, but I needed to see ye," she said softly.

"What is it?"

Serena glanced behind him where the mens' attention remained on her. Hunter must have seen her falter, because he grabbed her by the arm. "Wait." He pulled her outside and into the growing light of morning, away from the ears of any listening soldiers. His warm hand on her shoulder soaked through the chill. "Why'd ye come, Serena? This place isn't for ye." His eyes darted back to the lodge. "They may be lads, but they're dangerous like men."

"Mayhap I shouldn't have come, but I'm alone here, Hunter. I needed to talk to someone." Serena sucked in a breath of morning air. "I heard from the villagers about the sorceress who broke into the castle to kill the prince—"

"What is going on here?"

At the rough voice, Hunter pushed Serena. The sun pushed back the darkness in the east, tinting the dark sky a bright red and pink. In the dimness, Serena made out a familiar figure. She closed her eyes. "Not him," she whispered.

Milosh stepped into full view, his eyes resting on Serena. He frowned and swore. "What in the name of Thayer are you doing here with *her*, Hunter?"

Hunter flushed from the neck up. Serena's face grew warm when she realized what the prince must think, with her face so near Hunter's in the dark of early morning.

"Nothing, sire," Hunter said. "Nothing at all."

"I should hope not. If you are done here, come with me. The day is beginning." Milosh turned toward the castle, pausing as if waiting for Hunter to join him. "Come, master Hunter, your duties await."

Hunter didn't look at Serena, but followed the prince down the path toward the castle, leaving her cold and breathless.

And as Milosh and her brother sauntered away, she heard the prince say, "Maidens cause nothing but trouble, hear?"

Hunter turned over his shoulder and threw her a wink. "Aye, sire, I have it."

7

Darkness shrouded the hooded figures of the night as they stood under the safety of the forest. Black clouds hid the moon from view, and the rustle of the wind breathed through the last leaves of fall. A wolf howled in the mountains high above the shadows.

Enid shivered despite the warmth of her cloak as her companions spoke. Their cold voices told her what she had longed to hear since the first day of Thayer's reign, and excitement coursed through her veins. "When will you reveal yourself?" Enid asked. "My part of the bargain has been swung in motion. Now it's your time to act."

The Gifted Knights before her, who were stronger than her concerning the black magics, were expanding their giftings, growing stronger and more powerful than any mere mortal. Outcasts and rebels living deep within the mountains, they had been Enid's allies since the day Thayer claimed the throne.

"You have promised Prince Milosh dead," the leader of the Knights answered. "We hold back our hand until the stars align. Our power remains weak, but the time of the Marked is at hand. Soon King Thayer will know who truly holds command."

"The prince will soon be dead?" another Knight asked, leaning closer to Enid.

"Soon," Enid promised. "Soon King Thayer will begin to taste the pain that he has bestowed on the folk for so long."

✗

As a child, Hunter had believed in fairies and dragons, but Serena had pretended not to believe. Laughing at his antics, she hoped he'd see that the world held darkness, and he couldn't always play the hero.

However, when night fell and she lay alone under the furs on her cot, she chose to believe that one day all would be made well, that fairies danced in the moonlight and dragons roamed with their trainers.

Da had firmly tried to toss all such notions from either of his children's minds, but sometimes the Elders would give detailed accounts of mystic creatures in the country of Arnolein, or perhaps deep in the caves in Southern Sindaleer.

Serena always preferred the stories of the Lady of the Light who saved those who needed rescue and cured them of all ails. Her Light banished the darkness, and pain and suffering was vanquished.

And with these tales, Serena felt the hope that one day mayhap, just mayhap, the world would become a lighter place.

Sighing, Serena opened her eyes and let the warmth of her fur blankets slide from her body. Wolfe curled on her bare feet, and she playfully pushed him away. Darkness still shrouded the village, and with every breath she formed the white vapor of cold.

Time to make a fire.

Thundering hooves headed towards the village interrupted her thoughts. The mutts howled, and Serena's heart sank.

Not again.

Wolfe stirred, growling low in his throat. Serena threw her shawl over her shoulders, and slipped out into the cold. The mutt attempted to follow her, but she held up a commanding hand. "Stay."

The villagers had already gathered, pushing their way towards the direction of Bron where the soldiers rode from.

The elders held their spears, angry curses raining down.

"Times have grown darker for the king to not leave us alone!"

"May Thayer and his followers go to hell."

"They took our sons. All that is left is our lives."

Serena crossed her arms, fighting off the chill of fear and cold. Out of the corner of her eye, she caught sight of Clovis coming out of her hut. "What's going on?" Serena called out to her.

"I don't know. Mam sent me to go find out."

The two pushed through the villagers to the front of the fray, voices from the folk growing angrier as they drew near. A crowd of twenty or more villagers—men, women, children—gathered in a tight circle.

"Let me through!" Clovis said, her soft voice barely heard above the clamor. "What's going on?"

"It's one of *them*," a village lad yelled back. "Some of the soldiers found him doing it."

Serena began to push past the child, standing on tiptoe to see above the tall heads in front of her. Several soldiers dismounted, throwing a chained Sindaleerian to the dirt.

Her heart stopped as he rolled onto his back, the Marks visible on his wrists. *Nay.* She wanted to close her eyes to what she knew was to come, but imaginary chains wrapped over her, forcing her to watch.

"What is it?" Clovis demanded, hopping up and down, but to no avail.

The lad in front of the girls, sneered. "One with the Gift was caught usin' it. Now he's payin'."

The blood fled Serena's face. The villagers pushed and shoved her with dirty hands as she forced her way to the front of the crowd.

Her breath caught in her throat. The Gifted's brown hair hung long about his face, covering his eyes. Dirt and purple bruises marred his body. His torn tunic barely clung to his body, and he trembled in the cold.

"Everyone back!" a soldier yelled. Three of his men held up their spears, shoving folk several feet away.

Serena stepped back, her eyes still on the captive. His mouth moved, but above the angry murmurs of the villagers, she could hear no words. She only saw his wrists, the dark X's tattooed into his skin.

Tattoos like her own.

One of the soldiers strode towards his captive, thrusting his spear down towards his victim. The warrior was younger than Hunter, and despite the chill in the spring air, sweat dripped from his forehead, his eyes darting from side to side. A hush stole over the crowd.

The man with the Marks pushed himself up to his knees, swaying from side to side. He set his jaw. "Do it," he yelled. "Do it."

The soldier replied, but the words became lost in the wind. The folk cursed and screamed, cheering the young man on.

The Marked held out his palms to the young soldier. "Do it," he mouthed.

The soldier faltered.

"Do it!" the villagers chanted.

He faced the man with the Marks. A muscle ticked in his jaw, and his hand holding the weapon, trembled.

He threw down the spear. "I refuse."

Some of the villagers jeered, one man yelling out vile oaths.

The soldier, however, stood firm and began to walk away. His leader grabbed him by the shoulders and shoved him aside. Taking up the weapon from the dust, he crossed over to the Marked man.

Without glancing at the injured man , the leader slashed his wrists, twice each time to cut the X's, turned, and strode back to his horse without a word.

Blood pooled down the Marked man's wrists, dripping to the ground. He clenched his jaw, his eyes swinging to the young soldier who stood to the side.

Then, without a sound, his body hit the earth, his breathing labored as he fought through the pain.

Serena looked away, her own wrists aching.

Her heartbeat thrummed against her breast bone. Sweat trickled down her back. She couldn't help but see herself lying there beside him. They were the same.

He doesn't deserve to die.

8

Two days after the lads had arrived, Milosh had gathered them behind the barracks to show off their swordsmanship. The dark-stoned castle stood to their backs, and sunlight filtering through gray clouds with little warmth.

"Step up lads."

The youngest group held back, and Hunter knew they were far from ready to fight a skilled prince.

"Well, come on then," Milosh said, holding out a sword for one of them to take. As he raised his hand, his sleeve slid back, and Hunter caught a glimpse of a tattoo curling around the prince's wrist. The Serpent of Death.

One of the most feared mythical creatures in the Sindaleerian legends.

Hunter swallowed and glanced around. Seeing that no one stepped forward, he took up the sword from Milosh's outstretched hand. He had barely enough time to draw in a breath when steel clashed with steel. His ears rang.

Hunter ducked as the prince's weapon swung towards his shoulder. He dove clumsily to the left, dodging another aim, this time for his stomach.

Sweat beaded his upper lip.

Milosh stared him down, his eyes hard. *Come at me,* he seemed to silently mock.

Hunter thrived at archery, but Milosh made the sword-play of the villagers seem like that: play.

Hunter swung, but Milosh was faster. Steel against steel.

Locked gazes.

Heavy breathing.

Hunter swung around, breaking his sword free. He thrived in archery and ax throwing. The sword was like a foreigner speaking in a different language, a weapon taken seriously only when Thayer became king.

Milosh smirked. Before Hunter could blink or breathe, the tip of the prince's sword was at his throat. "Well, what do you have to say for yourself?" Milosh asked.

"What I learned in the village was horse's dung compared to what you can teach us." Hunter jutted out his chin. "Soon ye won't be able to keep up with me."

"The apothecary says he has one leg shorter than the other," Destin called out behind them. "Show him a little kindness."

Hunter shot Destin a look that he wished shot fire.

Milosh grunted, glanced around at the lads and nodded for Hunter to follow him to the castle. And just like that, with no explanation, Hunter became the manservant of the prince.

Each morning, Hunter rekindled the fire in Milosh's chamber, swept out the room, and wiped the prince's muddy boots. He woke Milosh, went down to the kitchen and brought him his breakfast, before helping his master dress.

Not exactly the tasks he would have imagined doing when he dreamed of gaining access to the castle. But he still received valuable inside information, and that made every moment worth the work he would have once scorned as 'for the woman-folk.'

Milosh rarely spoke to Hunter and he rarely talked back. The two spent entire days together without Milosh acknowledging him.

The silence both bothered and relaxed Hunter. His life at the village made him accustomed to quiet chatter, to the village's never-ending noises and continual companionship of one man or another.

Here at the castle in the city of Bron, he spent more days inside alone or outside with a silent Milosh as he trained the lads to fight—watching the lads do exactly what Hunter lived for: fighting and fighting well.

One evening as Hunter brought up the prince's meal, he found Milosh sitting back in a chair by the fire, his hand holding a crumpled piece of parchment. He glared up at Hunter as he entered the room.

"You're late."

Hunter glanced out the window as the sun made its descent over the crest of the mountain. Late? The prince was either being a prat or dumb. He'd arrived the same time ever since assigned the role of manservant.

Milosh cursed and threw the paper across the floor. "Who does he think he is?" he muttered, taking the plate from Hunter's hand and idly picking at the ham with his bare fingers. "No good son of a rat."

"Sire, I'm sorry, but this *is* the usual time."

Milosh didn't acknowledge that Hunter had spoken. He continued toying with the meat, before he grabbed a flask of wine and downed the liquid, throwing his plate on a table. "He thinks he can do as he pleases, make me a copy of himself, but to darkness with it all." Muttering curses, he drew his sword, picking another one up from a corner and handing the weapon to Hunter. "Come with me."

"Aye, sire."

He followed the prince out of his chambers, pretending that he knew exactly what Milosh planned to do. When they entered the stone courtyard of the castle, the prince turned, taking a fighter's stance. "Forget the pain in your leg. Come at me."

The sun hit Hunter in the face, blinding him for a long moment. He blinked, the prince blocked from his sight.

With a hard thwack, Milosh sent the blunt end of his sword crashing down on Hunter's shoulder. Before Hunter could react, he lunged again. "Come!" he muttered angrily. "Come back at me! Fight! Use your anger for strength!"

Hunter drew in a breath and hopped to the right to avoid another blow, ducking and trying to move closer. He swung the blade, steel clashing steel. The noise echoed in the soundless courtyard, sparks flying.

Hunter hopped back and almost toppled over. His back began to ache and perspiration dripped into his eyes, but he ignored the pain. Milosh took the respite to draw back and better prepare himself.

Hunter, however, waited until Milosh relaxed his arms, and dove forward, aiming for Milosh's stomach.

The blow fell short, and in but a breath, Hunter found Milosh's weapon aimed for his shoulder. He winced as the blade pricked skin before swinging back into the air, Milosh sliding the weapon into his sheath.

Hunter wiped his face, breathing hard.

However, Milosh appeared as though the fight had never happened. "Go back to the barracks and sleep. I don't need you anymore tonight." He turned. "Oh, and give that lass I saw you with a kiss goodnight for me." Then he headed for the barn, leaving Hunter standing in the courtyard looking after him.

Hunter wiped the blood from his shoulder where the blade had pierced through his woolen shirt. Milosh didn't fight like a man practicing his swordsmanship; he fought like a man battling his worst enemies.

And Hunter didn't plan on becoming one of those.

✗

Serena waited in the confines of her cottage until the rays of the sun disappeared behind the mountain, until the hum of the village grew to a peaceful hush. Her stomach failed to accept any food, and she paced the cottage, fighting to maintain a sense of calm.

However, her insides trembled as she waited and watched.

He couldn't have survived the brutal attack that had followed the slashing of his Marks, not now, not so long after he had lain in the dirt clinging to life. She had watched as the soldiers beat him, as life dripped from his body.

The village folk had all watched and done nothing, but no more. If Hunter could smuggle lads away from the king, she could save a dying Marked. Because that one man outside may one day be her.

As the light faded, she slipped outside alone, leaving Wolfe inside the cottage for fear he would give her away. The walk to the lodge dragged on as she became one with the shadows, her feet leading her behind cottages and around the two main barns.

Thank Destiny the mutts lay tied on the other end of the lodge, far away from the Marked man. She hastened her steps. Soldiers would be here soon to return for the body. They always did, to make sure the Marked would never breathe again.

The white ball of moon rose above the treeline, the cornfields beyond bathed in white light. She found herself running now. Were those horses' hooves she heard? Her quickening heartbeat took her breath away.

Her hand brushed the side of a deserted cottage as she rounded the corner. Her bare toes sank into soft dirt.

There lay the Marked.

Only paces from the lodge, a simple dark mass

on the ground. Kneeling down, she watched for the rise and fall of his chest, but the dim light of dusk hid him from view. Reaching out a hand to touch his face, she closed her eyes. She had touched death once before, and she hoped never to again.

However, warm flesh met hers, and she tried to hold onto hope. Glancing back at the village, she grabbed the Marked's feet and did the best she could do.

Dragging him may only do him more harm, but Serena knew she was in a race against life and death. In the end, either the soldiers would claim his life or she would. Back at her cottage, as night fell, dusk a distant memory, Serena bandaged the man's bloodied wrists. While the blood may have ceased, she knew that his damaged Marks should be the least of concern. For King Thayer, the cut Marks would be a sign to the folk that becoming more powerful than he would never be an option.

But the beating that followed had proven even more deadly. The bleeding of the wrists had stopped, but the inside of a person could forever be damaged. She watched the Marked's still face as she took a wet rag, attempting to clean a cut on his upper lip.

Ripping open his tunic and tossing the soiled rags to the floor, she sucked in a breath. His stomach and chest held purple bruises, deep cuts lining his torso and ribs. The man still lay in motionless sleep.

And now, as Serena brushed the hair away from his eyes, she saw that he could be no more than two summers older than she. His dark brown hair proved him to be a man of Sindaleer, and the small growth of a beard lined his mouth, but still she saw his youth.

The first young Marked she had seen since living in southern Sindaleer. "Do ye have the Gift of fire like the folk said?" she whispered, dipping her hand into some ointment to rub onto the cut above his eye. She expected no answer, but still she asked, "Do ye have family wondering what has become of ye?"

"What is *he* doing here?!"

Serena's heart caught in her throat and she whirled around, her hands glowing. "Hunter! What in the name of Destiny are ye doing here?"

Hunter's eyes remained on the Marked man. "I could ask the same of him."

Serena stood, cleaning her hands on her shift, her heart continuing its normal beat. "Ye need to stop giving me a fright every time we have a chance to meet."

"And I still want to know what a wanted Marked man is doing in the cot?"

"What do ye think I am doing?" Serena lowered her voice, pulling Hunter away from the doorway. "I don't like ye acting like this. This isn't like ye."

"My master is outside the village waiting for me to return with a dead Marked, Serena. I was looking all over for him, terrified it was ye."

Serena's heart softened. "I'm sorry, Hunter, but ye cannot be the only one to play hero. It is my turn tonight. I had no choice."

"Yes...but don't ye see? For so long we have been safe, but now ye bring him here, and this changes everything. What should I tell Prince Milosh?"

"Tell him the folk saw him crawl away into the

woods, tell him the Marked was too mangled to bring back so ye dropped him in a ditch."

"Serena." The way Hunter said her name made her pause. His voice changed, becoming more like a lad's than man's. "I'm scared. When I was searching the village, I thought for sure ye was the one dead. I've heard things that make me weak in the knees. The King will stop any of the folk who get in his way. I don't want to see ye being killed next."

Serena drew in a shaky breath.

"King Thayer is changing us," Hunter whispered. "I think war is coming and I don't want it to." He stepped toward the door. "I'm... I'm sorry, Serena. I'm scared. I'm not myself." His eyes pleaded with her. "Folk will find out..."

"They don't have to."

"But they will. I'll ask Destin to come. He'll get the Marked to the Guardians."

Serena reached for his hand, wrapping her fingers around his rough ones. "Please...keep a watch," she whispered.

"Hunter!" Milosh's voice rang in the darkness, causing Serena's heart to pause.

"I ... I have to go." Hunter glanced towards the door, his face pale. "I don't like this, leaving ye in danger. I don't like this change."

"Nay! Ye are in danger too. Please, be careful." She reached up, placing a kissing on his sun-darkened forehead.

With one final glance, he thumped his closed hand over his heart. *I. Will. Return.*

Serena smiled through her tears as his form disappeared into the darkness. This was one promise neither of them could keep now.

9

Serena watched the sleeping man's ashen face, the light of the candle illuminating the dark shadows around his eyes. His hair clung to his damp forehead, his chest rising and falling, at times just a whisper, from beneath the thin cover.

Her heart sank as she thought about Hunter's brief visit. About the sorceress that felt *she*, Serena of the village of Aedre, was the one destined to continue the line of Thayer with the prince

That she was the one the Seer had spoken of all those years before.

Serena studied the man slumbering before her. If she hadn't smuggled him away when she did, if it wasn't for the villagers' fear of touching a Marked, then he would be dead right now.

"What crime did ye commit?" she whispered.

"What did ye do, Marked?"

He moaned, and Serena resumed bathing his hands and neck, both still covered in blood and grime. Having him here with her in the cottage, felt foreign.

Serena always kept away from the men-folk, afraid to get too near, too attached. She found it easier that way, to pretend that she found more happiness with the women.

Because she knew, even as a small lass, that she would never marry.

No man would marry a Marked. Mayhap in the past, being a Gifted meant honor and renown. Mam had told her about the old days in which the folk sought the Gifted for wisdom, but that was long in the past.

She stood on legs sore from bending for so long, then laid the bowl of bloody water on the table. The cricket chirped outside the window, disturbing the quiet, beckoning her outside.

Rubbing her tired and aching eyes, she leaned against the doorframe, Her hands glowed, warmth pulsing through her body as she allowed a small ball of fire to rest in her hand. Eyes glazed, she stared at the flames. How dangerous could such a small fire be, or was Enid right and her Gift a dangerous weapon?

She remembered being a lass of eight summers and watching a little lad as the elders sentenced him for using his Gift. His screams had haunted her dreams for months after.

Mayhap that memory compelled her now to help the man lying on her cot.

"What…where….am I?"

Kara Linaburg

Serena snapped her hand shut, the flame extinguishing. The Marked man's eyes darted around the room and then to his bandaged wrists.

"Ye are safe here," Serena whispered, hurrying to his side. "Do ye remember the soldiers? The sentencing?"

"Nay, I don't...remember...anything."

Serena moved his blankets back around his bare shoulders. "The soldiers said ye were one of the Marked."

"Aye, I am." He closed his eyes and Serena thought he'd fallen back asleep. However, a moment later he opened his lids. "Thank you," he whispered.

Serena gazed down at her own wrists, covered by her sleeves. "Ye are most welcome."

✗

The rest of the night passed in a haze of dreams and reality. Serena floated in and out of sleep, slumped against the wall where she sat on the floor.

In her dreams, a man with curly hair atop a fine horse beckoned her to come. Then his head changed form as he took the shape of a monster, like the wraiths of the legends, and as Serena drew closer she saw that he held Hunter between his fangs.

Serena woke, the air sucked from her lungs. Milosh. She lay back against the wall, sweat running down her spine. The dream haunted her into the wee hours, and she slipped between waking and sleeping. Her mind whirled with thoughts of the man sleeping in the cot a few paces away and of Milosh, the man she'd been ordered to kill.

A noise caught her ear. Serena's eyes flew open, her hand reaching for the dagger in the hidden sheath of her moccasin. Crickets chirped outside the village, but above their chatter, fear pricked the back of her mind. She jumped to her feet, drawing the dagger and creeping toward the door.

The morning sun climbed above the mountain, the village astir. She saw and heard nothing unusual... except Destin leaning against the cottage wall smoking a pipe.

"Are ye now supposed to be at the castle?"

Destin grinned, letting out a puff of smoke as he did so. "So ye are the one keeping strange company now?" he asked quietly.

"Come in here before someone questions ye about why ye aren't working." Serena grabbed Destin by the arm and pulled him inside. Only months younger than Hunter, he often spent days at their cottage in times past, becoming more brother than friend to her and Hunter.

"Hunter sent me, remember?" Destin reached down to touch the ashes in the hearth. "Do you need me to relight the fire?"

"Nay, I'm fine."

Destin nodded his head to the stranger on the cot. "This him?"

"Aye."

"That was a risky thing you did, saving him and all. Most men wouldn't have dared such a foolhardy thing."

Serena's eyes narrowed, but she only nodded.

"Oi, don't be testy." Destin rubbed a hand over

his face. "It will take me three or four days to contact the guardians to get this one out. I needed to anyway though, 'cause Hunter told me that he and Milosh are going south in less than a month."

"They are?"

"Aye, to gather the lads like they did here."

Serena bit her lip, her heart settling in her chest, and shook her head. "I thought Hunter was a soldier in training for the king?"

"Nay, he's a manservant for the prince." Destin lowered his voice, leaning close to her ear so as to not be overheard. "Listen, we've already had one meeting for the smugglings since he joined up. We're planning to get fifty lads out of the south, mayhap a hundred by the end of the year. Hunter's work has just begun; it's a fortunate thing that Destiny brought us to the castle..."

Serena opened her mouth to speak, but Destin had already begun to examine the Marked man.

"Can you wait three days at least?"

Serena wanted to protest, but reason told her that Destin and his little band of smugglers could only do so much. She nodded, wrapping her arms around her as if to ward off the chill of the past night, but also to ward off the evil surrounding her land.

"I will be back in three nights." Destin shouldered his bow and quiver full of arrows, glancing back down at the wounded man. "Have him ready and let no one in. The men will be going out for the autumn hunts on the 'morrow. Your secret will be safer then." He stopped just short of crossing the threshold to the outdoors and gave her a small smile. "I admire you, sister.

Not many would be brave enough to do it."

"Aye ... but understand... Looking back, mayhap it was mere foolishness ... "

Destin bowed, his eyes holding approval. "Naw, Serena, I'd call it brave."

Without waiting for her reply, he disappeared like a wraith into the village, the animal skin on the door quivered in the wind. Serena shivered, her hands and feet numb from the cold.

Turning back around, she crouched down by the dry hearth, carefully stretching out her hands, allowing warmth to seep through her. She reveled in the sensation, closing her eyes, breathing in her Gift, letting fire flow through her veins. Then balls of flame flowed through her fingertips and into the hearth, lighting the cold wood.

The new fire crackled, the heat fanning her face. Closing her fingers, the light dimmed under her fingernails, and the fire in the hearth shone in the room.

Rising, she reapplied the healing poultice to the Marked man, carefully unraveling the bandages from around his wrists. He groaned as she reapplied the herbs, his tan face lined with perspiration.

"I don't know what ye are called," she whispered. "But I do know that ye have endured much and yet ye continue to fight. Ye are brave to stare into the jaws of death and continue to pull through. I know ye will live; hold on."

Serena went to the corner of the room, preparing leaves for tea, humming as she worked. Light began to stream through the lone window, a breath of fresh air to her tired body.

"Thirsty."

Serena whirled back around at the sound of his weak voice, drawing up a ladle of water. "Here. Drink slowly."

He nodded, most of the water running over his chin and onto his shirt as his eyes met hers. "Now aren't ya a ray of springtime in this cold world."

Serena ignored his obvious attempt to flirt. "I'm keeping ye here with me. In three days a friend is coming to get ye and bring ye to safety. Water will be beside ye here, and when I get home from picking apples, we'll eat some broth. Now, tell me, does anything hurt?"

The man nodded, his eyes closed.

"Can ye tell me where exactly?" She persisted.

"You mean, other than all over?"

Serena allowed herself to chuckle, dipping the ladle back into the bucket. "Well, aye, other than all over."

"I'm... I'm fine."

"And I'm Serena."

His eyes sparkled at her response, and she tried again, laughter in her voice. "Alrighty then, do ye feel any pain other than the usual pain of being beaten up?"

He shook his head, and she started to leave the bedside.

"Serena …?"

She stopped, turning to face him, his pale eyes watching her. "Yes?"

"I'm… Elston. Thank you."

10

Six years prior

"You ou want to be king—act like it." Milosh's father stepped away from the captive, placing a sword in Milosh's hands. "You want to be seen as worthy as my son, prove it.

Milosh's fingers closed around the cold steel. The two stood in the dungeon that stunk of human waste, death, and decay. His stomach turned as he watched the blindfolded man before him, his hands tied behind his back and to the wooden beam where he stood.

A Sindaleerian.

One of his fellow countrymen.

"It is easier," Thayer had said when he ordered the blindfold, "if you cannot see his eyes. It is easier the first time."

Milosh swallowed. He had killed in the south

81

before, shooting raiders who attacked his village. His blood ran loyal to Sindaleer—he was no stranger to death as a lad of four and ten summers.

But this was different.

The captive stood tall, his mouth set in a hard line. Even though he couldn't see his eyes, Milosh knew the man would show no fear. Folk in his country were taught not to fear death or pain, to stand tall in the face of torture.

But this didn't take away Milosh's own fear. He arched back his shoulders, praying his father did not see the hesitation.

Then Thayer gave the orders. "Kill him."

Miosh swallowed. His eyes remained open but without seeing—not really. He watched outside of his body, a bystander, detached from everything around him.

A ghost.

He lunged forwards, driving his weapon into the soft flesh of the Sindaleerian. Warm blood rushed out and over his hand. The man jerked back, and Milosh twisted the dagger deeper.

Deeper.

Deeper.

Until death claimed his father's traitor.

As Milosh stepped back, his hands and jerkin stained in an innocent's blood, a weight settled on his shoulders, and a crashing realization began to drown him.

He and his father were one in the same. He no longer stood a lad, guilt-free. Murderer. *He was a murderer.*

And there was no going back, not when you had crossed over the line to darkness. It had a way of claiming your soul, of stealing your sanity and all that you once saw as good.

✗

Present Day

Hunter leaned against the wall of the castle, sunlight warming the grounds, watching as Milosh trained the twenty or so lads recently taken from surrounding villages. The morning sun rose, chasing the fall chill from the air, the clash of steel echoing in the courtyard.

He remembered the prince's words the night before, the words that still sent his heart racing with fear.

"I just received word this eve from the king—I'm taking you and my men with me down south before the month is out. We're going to return with over a hundred lads for the king's army."

Hunter's stomach had twisted. *Nay.* "But sire, King Thayer has an army bigger than Minogloria's, and they too are feared. Why does he need lads when he has men?"

"Because, *master* Hunter, lads become men, and men trained from ladhood can be shaped and molded. You would not understand my father. No one does." He had spoken the latter under his breath.

"There's a war coming, isn't there, sire?"

"Aye, Hunter. A war no one is ready for."

Hunter's head snapped up from his thoughts as one of the lads groaned, falling to the ground and crying out in pain as his shoulder connected with the stone courtyard. Milosh loomed over him, his sword at the throat of the scrawny soldier in training. "You would be dead now if I were the bloody enemy. Get up."

The lad scrambled to his feet, his face pale.

Milosh pointed to the weapon on the ground. "Get it."

The lad nodded and grabbed the sword, holding the weapon clumsily in his hands. Without waiting for him to take a firm stance, Milosh swung the weapon in the air. Hunter winced as the dull blade thumped the lad on the shoulder. "Move!" yelled Milosh. "Move your feet!"

Fighting with the elders had never prepared the lads for Milosh's unpredictable hands. The lad licked his lips and ducked as the sword almost knocked him over the head. Milosh narrowed his eyes, his sword clashing once and then twice with the lad's until he had backed the poor lad up against the stone wall surrounding the castle's court.

The lad dropped his sword and Milosh stepped away, shaking his head with disgust. "Again."

And this was how training went with each of the lads the rest of the morning, as it had for the last weeks.

By mid-afternoon, the lads and Hunter filed into the barracks to eat a small fare of bread and mead, the soldiers grumbling about the prince and his unreasonable behavior.

"Always pushing us harder, like we're not warriors of Sindaleer," one said. "Back home, at eleven summers I killed a grizzly without blinking. Who does he think he is calling me weak?"

Hunter grabbed a tankard of mead, drinking half the liquid in one gulp. He swallowed. "Are ye sure ye didn't mistake the bear for a cub, Bjorn?" He smirked.

"You're one to brag." Bjorn tore off a hunk of bread, holding it between his thick fingers. "Suck up to the king."

"Braggart."

"Prat."

"Lame boy." Bjorn tossed a dough ball at Hunter, who stepped out of the way.

"Bad shot," Hunter said, snickering. He threw himself down by Bear, one of the few lads who hadn't seen him as the enemy once Milosh took him in.

"I hate it," Bear grumbled. "Milosh works us hard and then we have to deal with jacks back at the barracks."

"Who ye calling a jack?" Hunter said with quiet amusement.

Bear rolled his eyes. "You know what I mean."

"Milosh's too hard on everyone," another lad agreed, nodding to the taunting soldier. Hunter recognized the boy as one of the better fighters who stood a good deal shorter than the rest, but whose lightness and quick blows allowed him a place as one of the best in Milosh's eyes.

Hunter continued sipping the mead, watching the two as they discussed with the others what they disliked about the prince. Hunter wanted to join in, to say he agreed, but something stopped him.

Milosh may have pushed the lads and drilled them until exhaustion wore through, yet Hunter knew why. Mayhap he would be wrong in usual circumstances to force them to the limit, yet in this uncertain time in history Hunter remained conflicted.

He'd caught glimpses of the maps and battle plans Thayer forced the prince to study, and Hunter knew that Milosh didn't know whom they would one day face. In his unpredictable and often rough way, he'd slowly begun shaping them, preparing the lads for something much bigger than themselves.

"Are they shaping up, sire?" Hunter asked, as the evening fell and cast its shadows over the city of Bron. The prince had taken Hunter with him to the marketplace to have his bow mended and arrows made, and now they wove their way through the crowd toward the castle.

The smell of roasted pork being sold over a spit and hot applesauce, filled the air, mingling with the strong odor of unkempt bodies and horse dung. Hunter struggled to keep up with the prince's long strides as he avoided stepping into the piles of manure littering the stone walkway.

Milosh threw Hunter a bitter glance. "Aye. They're 'shaping up,' if that's what you call stumbling about. Thayer's army will never succeed."

"Aren't the lads part of yer army too?"

"What's that?"

Hunter nearly knocked over a basket of apples. "Sorry," he murmured to the old lady behind her stand. She touched his shoulder with a wrinkled hand and smiled.

Milosh glanced over his shoulder. "What is that you're saying?"

Hunter broke into a run to catch up, his back complaining with the sudden exertion. "The army is what ye have, what ye have been given to shape. Ye are commander, getting the lads and all that, training 'em. They respect ye." The lie slipped between Hunter's teeth before he could catch himself.

Milosh rolled his eyes at the words, and stopped by the maiden standing by the open fire with the roasted pork. "Two shares," he said.

The dark-haired lass handed him two steaming packages of wrapped meat. She bowed. "M'lord." Milosh nodded roughly. He reached into the skin pouch hanging from his belt and dropped ten buttons in her open palm. Her eyes lit up. "Thank you, m'lord."

Hunter was impressed. Buttons remained an article of value for seamstresses and the womenfolk, the rich buying them from traders in the south.

Milosh had made more than a fair trade.

Without a word, Milosh continued through the city square. "I bet the folk bloody respect me," he muttered under his breath. He stopped, turning to face Hunter. "Our King Thayer says the army is mine to control, but nothing is 'ours.' Nothing. Thayer owns everything, even the folk. They will not stand up to him.

They are weaklings, these peasants, cowards and a bunch of do-gooders.

"Do you know what it is like to be hated, to be dashed aside because of something that is petty and unimportant in your eyes? Do you know what it's like to have a cause you care deeply about to be snatched from you?"

"I—"

Milosh stepped back, his eyes dark. "I lived that bloody way until I was not much older than you, and my father finally wanted me." The word *wanted* rolled off his tongue like a curse word. "I had no one before that but my mam. And I would be a cursed half-wit not to take a chance at being something, and I will not let the chance of reigning go. Losing that dying Marked back at that village did not help matters—I thought Thayer would send me back to the dungeon after he heard."

The hate in Milosh's eyes caused Hunter to step back. The blood pounded in his temples, and he opened his mouth to reply.

However, Milosh didn't wait. He trudged back up the hill, through the second gate surrounding the castle. His jaw clenched. "Hunter..." For a brief moment, Hunter thought he wished to say more. Instead, the prince turned, his long strides taking him through the gate, up the courtyard steps, through the castle door, and out of view.

✗

Milosh walked straight toward his chambers, ignoring

Selwyn and the servants. He slammed the door behind him. No candles flickered on the table or windowsill, the fire cold in the hearth.

Darkness. All around him, nothing but the black void that threatened to swallow him.

He leaned against the stone wall, breathing.

In. Out.

A weight crushed his shoulders, wrapping around his insides. *Alone.* He stood alone.

He turned to the stone wall. A stone wall that may as well have been his life, holding him inside.

His hands closed into fists, the cold stone piercing him as he swung back. The blow brought him back to himself, but he swung again.

He hated that he'd brought his anger crashing down on Hunter. He hated that his mam's face rose every time he threw himself into a rage. He hated his father, the son of a rat who would bloody well never be a father to him.

He wanted to hurt the folk, the folk who called him "outcast" and "bastard." He wanted them to feel his pain, to understand that everyday he lived with the demons they could not see.

"That's not who you were created to be." His Mam's sweet voice haunted him, forcing him to draw back.

Sweat stung his eyes as he drew in a sharp breath. His fingers remained curled up in a fist, and pain shot up his arms whenever he tried to move them. The skin on his knuckles cracked, oozing blood.

He drew in another painful breath and stretched

his fingers out one by one. Nothing was broken… not this time, but he had now made holding a sword impossible for at least a week.

"Happy?" he asked himself.

Quiet was his answer.

He slid down the wall, cradling his hands to his chest, closing his eyes. He needed sleep, a sleep that would consume him and never let go.

Something folk called *death*.

Milosh leaned his back. He wanted nothing more than to sleep.

✗

Hunter rushed into Milosh's chambers. He'd heard the angry curses all the way from the stairwell. Serena's warning about an evil Marked remained fresh in his mind. The door hit the stone wall with a loud crash. "What's going on?"

Milosh sat on the floor, his knees up against his chest like a small child. He moaned, talking to himself, muttering incoherent words. In his short time at the castle, Hunter had already seen strange and angry outbursts from the prince, but nothing that had taken him so far from sanity.

"Are ye well?"

"Do I look well?"

Hunter's gaze traveled around the room and down to Milosh's bruised hands. "What happened?"

Milosh laughed hollowly. "I felt the bloody wall should be punched."

"Ye are crazy," Hunter muttered awkwardly, then

held out his hand, almost afraid of his master's reaction. "May I see?"

Milosh glared up at him. "I don't want you to hold my hand."

"Neither do I, stupid oaf. I want to make sure nothing's broken."

Milosh raised an eyebrow. "If you breathe a word of this to any of the lads at the barracks—"

Hunter held a hand over his heart. "Ye can behead me where I stand."

Milosh heaved a sigh and held up his hand. The cracked and bruised skin oozed blood, scabs of skin peeled back on his knuckles.

Hunter put pressure on the wrists, feeling for a break.

"Oi! Hunter, my hands hurt. Watch it!"

"Don't be such a lad. Lasses in my village know a thing or two about such injuries. My sister taught me a bit. Let me see."

Milosh grunted and mumbled under his breath. "Who do you think you are?"

"Who do ye think *ye* are?" Hunter stopped, realizing he'd spoken his thoughts out loud. "From the way your hand looks, I'd say the wall won this battle."

Milosh mumbled a curse under his breath and stood up, stretching himself out in a chair. Hunter held his breath, waiting for Milosh to roar back with more angry words and curses that would put to shame even the sailors in the south.

Instead, the prince smiled and shook his bruised finger at Hunter, wincing as he did so. "You have more guts than all of Thayer's army."

Hunter said nothing. He stuck out his chin and crossed his arms, trying to hide their trembling.

"You—" Milosh continued, "—need to be over my father's army. You would lead us to a glorious victory and send the enemy to hell with your gumption."

Hunter stayed silent, stepping back. "Ye have a sprain, sire, and won't be able to hold a sword for a good long while, but nothing snapped." He turned towards the fire, prodding it back to life. "I truly don't understand ye."

"How so?"

"One moment ye look as if ye may kill me and then the next ye laugh like a lunatic."

Milosh laughed. "I'll tell you this, Hunter, and if you spread this around then you will be seen in the village with your head on a spike. I've never had a servant and never wanted one. My father didn't require one of me and neither did Selwyn, the little devil. So you see, I chose you."

"Why? Ye said ye took me in because ye were getting threats… like that Marked trying to poison ye."

"Don't be as dumb as a donkey's behind." Out of the corner of his eye, Hunter watched Milosh lean against the wall. "You really think you could do anything to protect me? I lied, Hunter—your shocked expression is enough to make you look dumber than Selwyn. Do you not think I could defend myself? You and your shorter leg—why would I choose you? But your spirit, how you were never afraid. That fire in you despite the fact I still consider you a lad. You made me want to have you around me because I knew you'd treat me right."

The sparks in the hearth caught on the wood, and Hunter straightened. "You make me sound like a weak maiden."

"See there." Milosh smirked. "You prove my point, Hunter. You spoke to me as if I were part of your village and not your prince."

Hunter sucked in a breath. Milosh's argument struck a chord inside him. The prince's hatred for their government. For the king. For all that Thayer stood for.

That fire of rebellion that burned in Milosh could be used for the good of the Sindaleer, for the rebellion Hunter longed for.

Careful, he cautioned himself. *Tread carefully.*

"Have ye ever thought that ye could defy what everyone else thinks? Did you ever imagine being more than what the folk assumed you were?" Hunter asked.

Milosh raised his eyebrows. He threw himself down on a chair, and propped his legs up on the table. He stuck his dagger in a nearby apple. "Are we speaking treason?" He paused, glaring at Hunter. "I could have you hung for asking me that."

"But what if ye could save lives, turn the tables. Ye don't have to be who the folk say ye are." *An arrogant prat.*

Milosh said nothing and his eyes hardened. Still Hunter persisted.

"Ye have an advantage in this place to make a difference. Ye can do more. Ye don't have to become yer father and give the folk the satisfaction of being right—"

Milosh jumped up so quickly Hunter stumbled

backward in surprise. The chair clattered to the floor. Milosh crossed the room in four giant steps, grabbing him by the scruff of the collar and pinning him against the wall. His eyes blazed with fury. "If you ever speak of this again, I swear you will not live to see another day. I will *never* be my father." Milosh let go, rubbing his bruised hands as he stalked out of the room.

||

"*Take... care of...*" *Mam gasped from where she lay on the cot. The fire cast shadows over her pale face. "Promise me... ye'll take care of yer brother..." Her hot hand touched Serena's face. Sweat beaded her forehead, and Serena wiped the moisture away with a wet rag.*

Mam wrapped her fingers around Serena's wrist. "Promise me," she pleaded. "No... fire..." Her words came out in soft gasps, and she coughed, her body shuttering. "Serena..."

Serena blinked back tears. "Mam, yer staying right here."

"Nay... promise..."

Serena tapped her fist over her heart. "I promise."

The sickness had come without warning, shadowing Sindaleer and the lands surrounding. Some said the merchants had brought it back from over the seas, others said it was a curse.

Da passed onto the great beyond first.

Mam followed three days later.

Death. So much death.

Serena had dragged their parents to the mass graves alone. Nearly all the folk were ill or tending their own. There was no ceremony. No way to commemorate loved ones.

Just a mass grave where some of the lads burned the bodies each night, the smell of flesh and disease causing Serena to vomit.

And then Serena had almost lost Hunter. His young body had shook with chills and fever, and he was too weak to speak for days. However, amongst all this, for one thing Serena remained grateful: he never remembered their parents' deaths. Never had to see their unseeing eyes. Never had to watch their bodies lay among the others who had passed onto the great beyond.

For that she would be eternally grateful.

But in those terrible months of the accursed sickness, Serena had *seen, and their dead faces haunted her nightmares long after. And she vowed that nothing would become of her brother. He was all she had left in this world, and she would do whatever it took to keep him safe, no matter the cost.*

✗

Present Day

Serena watched the bread bake over the fire, out of habit allowing little bits of fire to spark from her fingertips, playfully shooting them towards the ground. Warm energy encircled her as she concentrated on the Gift.

And this time, instead of simply flames, little animals made of tongues of fire danced in the air, hovering above her hand. A little puppy chased his tail, a wolf howled at the moon, and a fish leapt out of a stream before the three disappeared into the fire below, mixing with the other orange flames.

Serena smiled, the light illuminating the whole room.

"So you have it, too?"

Serena's hand closed, and she turned, her gaze meeting Elston's.

"Aye."

Elston nodded. "I thought as much. You have the look of one."

"How so?"

"Your kindness to someone who is different, to someone who deserves death. That proves it. No one I know back home would have done it. The folk in this country seem to be bent on killing those who don't look worth it... Of course I don't know if I deserved another chance."

"Ye did *not* deserve death."

"You don't know me." He let out a low laugh. "If you did, you may have let me die."

Serena stood, pouring some water into a kettle to hang over the fire for the tea. "I don't believe that for a moment."

97

Elston grinned, his pale face. "The gift of fire is a wonderful thing. Wish I had it."

Serena placed the kettle on a metal hook over the hearth. "What Gift do ye have?"

"Stories. I make them come alive"

"Stories?"

"Aye, stories." Elston smirked. "Ya know, those things you tell the lad and lasses around the fire? Except, when I say alive, I mean, I can't just make a real dragon suddenly appear, but sure as I'm standing here, it seems real. 'Course, I have been known to make real rain and snow from time to time."

Serena sprinkled tea leaves over the boiling water. "Is that why ye were almost killed? Because ye told a story?"

Elston glanced away, the jest disappearing from his bruised face. "Mayhap," he said finally. "Mayhap it was." His eyes grew dark before brightening with false happiness. "Now then, are ye always working? Do you never have fun, Springtime? Other than rescuing poor wounded lads like myself, I mean."

Serena smiled faintly, trying to decide what she thought of his nickname for her rolling so easily off his tongue. "Aye, I used to work at the castle when I was a young lass... But since my Mam and Da died, I took care of my brother and sold the things I sewed in the marketplace in the city."

"So getting wed is out of the question? Being a normal lass and having fairly normal wee ones?"

Serena's cheeks flushed at his directness as she focused on the onion, chopping each piece into fine bits.

"Being Marked means that ye are never *normal.*"

"Marked can marry Marked, though, right? You could wed me. I could always use a lass as pretty as you are to cook me my meals and tend to me. I mean, after I go into hiding with those grizzly Guardians, life is going to get pretty tiresome. Plus, with my looks, we'd make handsome kids..."

"Aye, ye are a right tease ye are." Serena tried to speak in jest, but found a tightening in her chest. "I cannot marry any man, not here. I may only bear him Marked ones, and where would that leave them?"

"Why not leave? Why not flee the country?"

"Because... because Hunter... And once we almost went, but I said no, and there's that." Frustrated, Serena realized tears teased her eyes.

Elston cocked his head to the side, his eyes growing warm. "Hey, don't worry, Springtime. You know what happens in all the fairy tales I've heard, about the lowest of the lowest maidens? They always marry the prince."

"There's about as much chance of seeing that as of the Marks being worshiped."

Elston laughed. "Not a chance, huh?"

Hunter ran along the road, glancing over his shoulder. No moon hung in the sky tonight. The land lay covered in a blanket of darkness.

Somewhere in the distance a mutt barked. Hunter

picked up speed, leaping over more fallen trees and a little stream that gurgled beneath him. If he failed to return before too long, then his life would be forfeited. He'd already angered Milosh once, and he couldn't do it again.

That evening the prince had watched him more closely; all the documents were now locked in the secret compartment in his wardrobe, the key around his neck.

The sinking feeling in Hunter's stomach only deepened. He'd lost the little trust from the prince he'd earned over the last few weeks, and he didn't think he'd be able to earn back that trust anytime soon.

A flash of light glowed in the distant horizon. Hunter scrambled up a rock and jumped off, almost twisting his ankle in a hole. He bit his lip to keep from crying out, ignoring the pain as he plodded on.

Fell and Destin already sat around the fire, smoke rising up into the dense thicket of treetops above. Nick leaned against a tree away from the light, his eyes closed. Another lad used his knife to carefully carve something into a little stick he held in one hand.

A tall stranger stood in the shadows, his eyes resting on the Northern Mountains. A black cape hung over his tall form, making him almost invisible in the dusk. He held a longbow in one hand, the weapon of choice for most Guardians.

Fell let out a low whistle and Hunter returned it. He crept into the clearing and into full view of the smugglers.

The stranger turned, his eyes glowing in the firelight. Hunter nodded in greeting, and the man crossed the uneven ground in a few short steps, clasping Hunter at the elbows and bowing his head slightly in the Guardian greeting. "Master soldier," he said softly.

"Master Guardian," Hunter returned in greeting.

As the Guardian turned away, Hunter heard him lament to himself, "All so young to be part of the rebellion."

Together the smugglers sat around the fire, Nick and the other young lad scooting closer. Fell crossed his legs, a smoking pipe hanging from his mouth. "I called this meetin' because Destin asked me to. He said Hunter had something he wished to speak of. Hunter?"

Hunter stood. "I have news that ye'll all like. I know when and where the next pickings for the lads in the south will take place."

Thankfully, Milosh had talked of this before Hunter managed to destroy all trust between them.

"I plan—" he continued, "—to go ahead and get them out. If I go now, I can get fifty or more to safety with some Southern Guardians."

Fell shook his head. "Send someone else, lad. The prince will know it's ya instantly. You can't do that. We need you at the castle, and by going you'll be putting your life at risk. You'll be deemed a traitor."

"But I have to do this! Thayer's planning an army for Destiny knows what, and we need to weaken his plans. I'll make that sacrifice if asked of me, but he won't catch me or the lads, and he won't know about the other smugglers."

"I'll go. There's no one else. I've seen the maps myself, and I've lived in the south."

The Guardian lowered his hood, his dark hair pulled back with a leather thong. He quietly studied Hunter. "I will call for my Guardians around Sindaleer. They shall go—not you."

Hunter pleadingly glanced at his leader, begging him not to agree, to let Hunter help, but Fell ignored him, nodding in agreement. "Copy the plans, Hunter, and give 'em to Destin. He will get them to me."

Hunter ground his teeth in frustration, but arguing with Fell would do no good. "Aye, tomorrow I will get ye the plans."

"Good, then we agree? You'll follow orders and not suddenly go and do somethin' foolish?"

Hunter shifted uneasily at the penetrating stare of the old man and reluctantly nodded in silent agreement.

Because he didn't plan to listen.

✗

Lavender and herbal essence. Droplets of thick blood tainting her skin. The knife hovered over the sleeping form. Her hands shook.

"Do the deed," a voice whispered out of the darkness. "You have no choice."

Her hands shook as she raised the weapon, a scream erupting.

"Serena!"

Serena's eyes flew open, her chest heaving. She withheld another scream.

"Serena, what's wrong?"

A mutt howled in the distance. From the high

window, she could see the darkness and the flicker of
stars.

"I'm fine, Elston. Ye can go back to sleep. A... a
dream... just a dream..." She heard the cot creak as Elston
turned back over.

Raising her hands, she breathed a heavy sigh. No
blood. She was safe.

"Believe the lies," her mind whispered back.
"Enid wasn't a crazy witch. She'll keep her promise and
return."

Serena turned over, burying her feet deeper into
Wolfe's fur from where he slept at the end of her bed and
ignoring the voices she knew spoke truth. The steady beat
of the drums from the lodge pulsed through the night, and
she shivered.

Elston's cot creaked. Through the darkness, she
could feel his eyes on her.

"A long time ago," Elston began. "A lass wished
to find her purpose in this dark world, but her Gift was
small. She could only make Light, and light could not do
much. She could do nothing but shine light, and that felt
very small while her country was at war."

Suddenly the sounds of battle and death and rage
and pain echoed in the once quiet room. Serena glanced
up from where she lay, watching Elston's dark form.

"And the folk shunned her because her Gift
seemed too small, and she could do nothing to help in the
war," he continued. "But what the folk never realized was
that her light was pure and untouched... that her light
could heal all those who accepted it. They didn't realize
that the lass could penetrate the darkest of hearts, if only

they let her in." And a beautiful light lit the room, glistening in the dusk.

"And one night, the evil lords of the land tore through the village and drove her and the folk away, leaving the lass Ardara an outcast, poor and alone in a cold forest with no folk around her." A drop of cold wet something touched Serena's nose and cheeks. Snowflakes.

"So," Serena whispered. "She made it her mission to create a world of light and beauty, a place of healing."

"And the lady passed onto legend as the years went by," Elston whispered. "But she lives on in the memory of the Gifted folk who are now shunned as she is, as well all who wait for the Gifted to rise again." His voice faded, and he turned his face from her.

"I always loved that story," Serena said. The beat of the drums returned, the snow evaporating and with it, the magic of Elston's story. "I only wish I believed she existed, that somewhere she's waiting for the moment when we can rise again and together banish the darkness in the land."

"But you rescued me, didn't you?" Elston asked. "Mayhap her light resides in each one of us. Mayhap it is up to us to carry on the light." He paused. "So are ya ready to raze the castle to the ground? I mean with your fire and my bloody good storytelling, we'd be unstoppable."

Serena laughed. "Go to sleep, Elston."

"Goodnight, Springtime."

"Goodnight, silly lad."

✗

Serena folded up the beaded dress into her satchel. She could feel Elston's eyes on her from where he lay on the cot, relaxed, as if he did not have a care in the world, as if the king wasn't out *hunting* for his head.

"I'm taking this dress to the market in Bron," she told him. "I hope it'll fetch a good price. Mayhap I can trade it in exchange for flour or warm blankets for winter." She pulled her cloak over her shoulders, glancing down to be sure her Marks remained well hidden behind her sleeves. "I should be back by supper. How do yer wrists feel?"

Elston smiled and shrugged. "They hurt, but I'll be fine. No worse than the time I wrestled with a dragon and his claws tore a chunk off my shoulder."

"A dragon? *Really?*" Serena raised her eyebrows.

Elston laughed. "See ya later, Springtime."

Serena bade Wolfe stay behind with Elston, before heading through the village towards the bustling city. The day passed by with more luck than she hoped for, and the dress fetched a good price. She returned to her cottage that evening with both flour and a knitted blanket from a local farmer, her heart full.

When she pulled back the fur hanging over the cottage door, the sharp smell of burning caused her heart to lurch. The last thing she needed was her cottage to catch fire with Elston inside and the village folk running to her aid.

Hurrying inside she almost collided with the man

himself.

"Serena! You weren't supposed to be back yet."

"What are ye doing?" Serena glanced around at the smoke filled cottage and back to Elston's amused expression. He held up a plate of baked bread—at least that is what she assumed the blackened form was.

"I'm baking supper," Elston said, sitting his creation on the table and crossing his arms. Then he winced, quickly uncrossing them. "I forget my wrists." His eyes sparkled out from under his tousled hair, the bruises on his jaw now a painful black.

"Ye are baking supper," Serena repeated, unable to hide her own amusement.

"Aye, now sit yourself down and eat this grand and mayhap a bit blackened—but nonetheless tasty—meal." He awkwardly pulled up a stool, taking care to not move his wrists this time. He motioned for her to sit. "And speaking of you being away, how was your luck with that dress?"

"All went well," Serena said, glancing down at the mush in the bowl before her. "What is it that ye have made?"

"Stew with bread fresh from the fire." Elston pulled up a seat beside her, his eyes expectant. "Well?"

Serena dipped her spoon with slight hesitation into the brown mush before her, and took a sip. The warm broth settled in her mouth, the taste surprisingly pleasant. The flavor of carrots from the summer and dried venison caused her mouth to water. "It's... it's good." She took another bite, her eyebrows raised. *Now, I fear the bread may be a wee bit unfortunate.*

"You sound surprised." Elston stuck out his lip. "Ya pain me, lass, underestimating my talents." He took a bite of his own stew. "Why, it's better than I thought it would be," he admitted with a light laugh.

Serena smiled back, the heat from the stew mingling with another kind of heat... the pleasant sensation from Elston's kind gesture. "Ye didn't have to do this, Elston."

"Nay, I wanted to. Ya saved my life. This is just a small thing I could do to show how glad I am to still have my head attached to my shoulders." He lowered his voice. "And mayhap, just mayhap, you'll reconsider my marriage offer after this meal."

At first Serena's heart lurched with his flirting, until she caught the tease lurking in his warm eyes. "Aye, not a chance. Ye make good stew, but your bread is a bit lacking." She gestured to the lump on the table. "Ye still have a wee bit of improvement to do."

✗

And just like that, when for the first time she found someone who understood, the sweet time ended, disappearing as all good things seemed to be doing in the land.

Right at the moment before the peak of night came and the moon rose high in the sky, Serena heard the shuffling of feet and a low whistle outside the door. Destin.

He stepped over the threshold, drawing back the hood of his cloak and shaking his hair like a wet dog.

"It's raining out, and a mite chilly for fall."

He paused, shivering and rubbing his arms to ward off the chill. Glancing over at Elston, he said in an undertone, "Get up, Marked. Time's wasting."

Elston's wounds still hindered much movement in his hands, but he felt cool to the touch as Serena helped him get to his feet. He glanced down at her, his eyes twinkling. She warmed, aware of how his shoulder brushed hers.

Elston bowed towards Destin. "I'm Elston. Thank you for coming."

Destin nodded. "Nice to know you. I'm glad to meet any enemies of the king, but right now we better hurry. I'm on guard duty in a few."

Elston took a step forward, swaying slightly. Serena reached out a hand to steady him, but he waved her away. "I'm fine." He pulled on his boots that were set by the bed and nodded his thanks as she handed him his pack, a grin lighting his face. "It was a pleasure being tended by a lady such as yourself, Springtime."

He bent down and kissed her on the forehead. She felt his soft lips down to her toes, the gentle caress lingering. And just as quickly, he straightened, his eyes warm. "I will repay this kindness someday. Keep that in mind." His breath fanned her face, and he winked. "I may save your life. Returning the favor, ya know?"

Serena's face flushed and out of the corner of her eye, she saw Destin observing them. "Just be a Guardian and save the good folk of this country. That's all the thanks I need."

Her smile wavered with the tightening of her

chest. She'd known all along that he couldn't stay here, but a piece of her wished that things were different, wished that their Marks didn't define them… that folk like Thayer and Milosh were only figments of her imagination.

Destin and Elston turned to the door, but Elston stopped, glancing over his shoulder. "And keep those lads away, Serena. Tell them you got a future Guardian looking after your hide now."

Serena nodded, the lump in the back of her throat growing. She watched as the two disappeared into the shadows, Hunter's mutt brushing against her legs.

Elston glanced back once, his hand lifted in farewell.

And she knew that she would never see him again.

12

The next morning, Hunter left the barracks, heading for the castle. Ever since he'd spoken the traitorous words to the prince, Milosh treated him as coldly as he did the other villagers. The two of them had never been friends, but still Hunter loathed the prince's dark looks and harsh orders.

Hunter crossed over the threshold and into the castle when a soldier came hurrying through, almost running Hunter down. When he saw him, he grabbed Hunter's shoulders to steady himself. "You're needed in the prince's chambers double quick."

Hunter didn't wait to hear more, and bounded through the hall and up the stairs. He threw open Milosh's door and stopped short.

Food lay on the floor, the scattered remains of meat, bread, and wine in a blood-red mess. Milosh leaned against the fireplace, blowing into his pipe. Hunter met Milosh's sullen glare. "What happened?"

Milosh took his pipe out of his mouth, drawing in a lungful of clean air. "I was almost poisoned," he said in disgust.

Hunter knelt down to touch the food remains, but Milosh put out a hand. "Stop! I said it's poisoned. The poison could enter your blood, or so the apothecary told me. I suppose his bloody word can be trusted," he muttered. "He'd be the only one I could trust around here if that's true."

Hunter withdrew his hand to wipe on his pant leg as if he'd already touched the liquid. "When did this happen?"

"This morning. The food smelled funny and I refused to eat it. I summoned the cook and asked her what had happened. She trembled and said it was nothing, but I still pressed her." Milosh drew in a sharp breath. "She said that a lady had come to her and told her that if she didn't use the poison, she'd kill her daughter. The cook said that the lady proved her Gift by inflicting upon her a terrible pain—one that could only come from someone with one of the Gifts. Thayer sentenced the cook to a whipping and then to three days in the dungeon."

Hunter swallowed, trying to hide his disgust at the mention of the prince's father.

Milosh sat down. "I know who did this."

"Who?"

"The lady who came into my chambers some time ago. Since she didn't succeed the first time, I believe she is continuing her mission."

Milosh swung his feet around and stood, going

over to the wardrobe and rifling around in the back. When he turned around, his face had grown hard. "Thayer wants me to go over the map, see our destinations and travel plans," he said more bitterly. "Put gloves on and clean up that bloody mess."

✗

Serena's dreams ate at her mind. Enid's icy fingers gripping her shoulder, Elston's flirty wink, Milosh's cold stare.

And then the scene changed. In her hand, she held a silver dagger with a golden handle, the tip dripping blood. A cold laugh escaped her throat.

Fingers reached out, closing around her throat, choking her, cutting her off from life's air.

Her eyes flew open, the dream vanishing. Morning glowed pink outside the cracks around the doorframe, and the world around her finally became real.

However, the hand around her throat remained.

Nay. Not a dream.

Serena opened her mouth to scream, but only a muffled squeak escaped. Wolfe barked before falling silent.

Her foot contacted something hard as she tried to kick, but her captor didn't move. The sharp scent of lavender met her nose.

Enid. The tip of her dagger edged closer to Serena's bare neck. "Silence. I told you I would return."

"I... I..."

"Surely you see that we must act, that if no one

112

will stand up for injustice, we must." Enid leaned back, and Serena could clearly see into the sorceress's eyes for the first time, surprised to find vulnerability mingled with hate and fear.

"Why... Why do you want me to do this?"

"You will fulfill the prophecy, and King Thayer deserves to feel pain, to feel the things he loves taken away from him one by one. He killed my son and I will return the deed with vengeance. I have waited years for this moment, and now that he has taken Prince Milosh into his castle, treating him as a beloved son, the time is now.

"First to die will be King Thayer's son, then his kingdom." A fevered shadow fell over Enid's face. "Prince Milosh's father has caused us all pain—you with your Marks and all others who bear them."

Elston's face danced in Serena's mind, the blood draining from him as the soldier raised his sword.

"It should not bring you too much pain to kill him," Enid finished, sheathing her dagger, and talking as though she spoke of nothing more than the weather. "But I know you are soft-hearted, and so I brought you this." Slowly she reached up and withdrew from her neck a long necklace which shimmered in the morning light. A gold medallion swung gently back and forth on a black ribbon, harsh symbols engraved on the rim.

Enid glanced down, murmuring low words in a tongue Serena didn't understand. Then the witch forced the necklace into her hands. "This will kill the bearer. I have placed its curse, Serena. I will find you if you return without Milosh dead. Put this medallion around his neck

113

and in less than a day he will be too weak to move, fading into the most unimaginable death. I will know if this necklace does not have a bearer."

Then Enid was gone.

Chills crossed up and down Serena's legs. Wolfe lay sleeping on the floor. She swallowed, her throat dry like a late summer's day. "Some watch mutt ye are."

And yet, if she did not have the necklace in her hands, she would have sworn this was another one of her nightmares.

The sick smell of lavender lingered, teasing her fear as she rolled over, trying to block out the world.

✘

Two days passed and the thought of the maps in Milosh's wardrobe did not abandon Hunter. He couldn't bring himself to try and break in. He could only imagine Milosh finding him, checking the documents at night and somehow knowing that Hunter had copied them.

Milosh examined the documents every night, studying the faded markings that Thayer had drawn, trying to memorize the best routes, and adding up the number of lads. He would send soldiers ahead to the nearest villages and would go himself to the southernmost ones near the ocean.

Soon.

On the third day, Milosh stood in the tower in the wall surrounding the castle, his face towards a huge open window. The tower stood at the foot of the gate where folk entered and left the castle. Darkness began to fall like a curtain, shadows lingering over the prince's weary face. "We leave tomorrow."

Hunter's heart sank in his chest at the curt words. His fingers curled into a fist. He nodded.

"I loathe taking the lads," Milosh said.

"Just as much as ye scorn the peasants?"

Milosh laughed, but the hollow sound held no humor. "I do not scorn them for no reason, Hunter."

"Ye give the impression that ye hate them."

"Yes." Milosh leaned out toward the city, clasping the walls to keep from falling over. "I do at times. I don't deny it. They took everything from me, and my anger—" He shook his head. "I want to unleash it on something, to let someone feel the pain I have for so long. I admit, it's gotten the best of me…"

"It's more than ye who feels that pain."

Milosh turned, the hood of his cloak shielding his face. "Who?" For the first time since the night of his violent outburst, he sounded curious about what Hunter had to say.

"Well…" Hunter leaned against the wall, wondering if he'd said too much. "Those Marked that your father wants killed? Those lads that ye capture and hold as prisoners? Those are the ones who have nothing because of who they are and..." Hunter drew in another sharp breath. "Ye don't care."

He left without waiting for Milosh's answer. His heart slammed against his ribs as he turned through the door, racing down the steps. He paused near the bottom, waiting to hear the following footsteps of an angry Milosh.

But only quiet roared against the blood pounding in his ears.

The prince would surely kill him now, or at least throw him out of the castle where he would have no access to the parchments.

Hunter had no choice—he was leaving.

13

Dim light streamed into the cottage. Serena pushed back the flap covering the doorway to step outside, almost colliding with Clovis. Her friend stepped back, Wolfe yapping at her heels.

"Back, Wolfe," Serena said, glancing down. Her wrists were covered, and she had made the fire before dawn. All was well.

The sun hadn't yet risen above the trees, and work had just begun at the castle. Serena herself had been heading to the wood to check the traps by the river. Her friend turned her worried face towards her. A rock settled in the pit of her belly. "What's wrong?"

"Have you heard from Hunter?"

"Nay, not for a long while."

"He's gone," Clovis whispered.

"What?"

"Aye. He's gone. I heard the news in the castle. I saw Milosh for the first time, but he was not at his best.

117

He ran from his chambers muttering curses that would make a pirate blush."

"But what happened? Where's Hunter?"

"I know not for sure, but Milosh says—and I gathered this from the servants—that Hunter stole two maps from his chambers and is going south. Now Milosh is going after him—alone."

The breath fled Serena's lungs. "How does he know it was Hunter who stole the maps?"

"I know not, but I suspect that has something to do with an outburst of Hunter's in the tower at the castle gate. The maids—"

She paused, glancing up as Serena reached for a pack hanging on the wall. "Wait! Where are you going, Serena?"

Kill the prince. Enid's voice echoed in her mind. *He deserves to die.*

She ran over to the lone cupboard on the wall opposite the door and stuffed in the remainder of the jerky and some hard bread. She grabbed the bucket from the table, poured the water into a drinking pouch, and sealed the mouth.

"I need to get to Milosh before he finds Hunter." She pointed to Wolfe. "Keep the mutt safe?"

"Of course, but Serena, I don't understand. This isn't like you! You must be reasonable and realize you can't do—"

Serena tried to calm her racing heart. "Ye are right, this is not like me at all, but I *can do something. I can't* let Hunter die."

Kill the prince.

The medallion still lay like a heavyweight in her pouch looped through the belt around her waist. Her hand reached down, brushing against the leather encasing the murder weapon. She would use the medallion—*must* use it—if only to keep her baby brother safe.

Clovis stood blinking by the doorway, her face twisted. "I don't understand."

Serena swung her leather bag over her shoulder. "Aye, I know, but I'll return and ye will. In the meantime, take care of Wolfe?"

"Aye, but Serena, Milosh will ki—"

"Nay." Serena took her cape from the peg on the wall, her throat tightening. "Do ye know where Hunter would go first?"

"South is all Milosh said. I... I think he's going to the lower villages. I... I overheard him telling his da's advisor."

"Milosh will take the main road," Serena decided aloud. "It's faster. Farewell."

The wind slapped at Serena's face as her horse gathered itself under her, flying across the flat ground. Her lips remained stiff with cold, shivers of excitement and fear mingling throughout her body.

Hunter. She'd kill him if Milosh didn't first.

Her heartbeat matched the pounding of the hooves. Freedom. Freedom. For the first time she tasted freedom—freedom from the village, freedom from herself.

The prince going after her brother had decided for her what sleepless nights in her cottage couldn't.

Clouds raced across the sky, shielding the sun. She slowed her mount three times that morning, resting and stretching her limbs. By evening, her legs grew stiff with exhaustion.

She lit a small fire after wearily gathering sticks, placing them near a huge stone wall that she hoped would shield her from the cold. The fire barely coursed through her fingers before she flung herself down on the hard ground, pulling her cape tighter around her weary body, and drifted into a restless sleep.

Mam's face drifted into her dreams. *"Serena,"* she whispered. *"Keep your brother safe... promise..."*

Serena's eyes flew open. She lay curled in a ball, the quiet of the night assaulting her ears.

A branch cracked.

Serena sat up. The fire remained only glowing ashes. Around her, darkness swarmed.

Another crack. Serena's stiff hands fumbled for the dagger in her moccasins. Her fear grew with each beating of her heart. A crash echoed through the forest's dense underbrush.

Serena gasped, yanking the dagger out of its sheath and jumping to her feet. "Who's there?"

Silence.

Serena stepped forward, making her way beyond the light of her dying fire and into the surrounding trees. Nothing amiss. No more sounds. She was alone.

Drawing in a breath she walked several more paces until her camp was only a small light in the distance.

'Twas only an animal, Serena, ye should know better.

She walked a few steps further, but finding nothing, turned as if to go back. A spark of orange turned her attention to the trees beyond her camp. She glanced again. Yes, there was the flicker again, a light of a fire.

Hunter?

She crept along through the brush, briars tangling around her dress and cloak.

The fire crackled and smoke drifted around the silent night. A sleeping form lay on the ground wrapped in a blanket.

Serena bit her cold lips, uncertainty stinging. She didn't recognize the figure, but if friend or foe, it didn't matter. She alone with only her dagger could do very little.

She turned as if to retreat, but a crack from a stick under her foot sent her heart to the forest floor. The clenched dagger in her hand wavered.

A breath of pause.

Then the form jumped up from the ground, fitting an arrow to his bow and turning around. The deadly point of the arrow directed to her heart as the bowman's eyes connected with hers in the darkness.

Serena sucked in a painful breath, and closed her eyes. *Nay. Please. Anyone but him.*

Milosh.

"Come out of the shadows." His rough voice shook the still.

Serena took a step as if to obey, but suddenly

whirled back around. Before her brain could catch up with her feet, she found herself running blindly through the trees, hoping that Destiny would allow the arrow to miss her in the dark.

"Oi! Wait!"

His shout only propelled her faster. Briars and thorns grabbed at her legs. She flew through the wood, ducking under low hanging branches and leaping over a log. She could hear him behind her, shouting curses as he ran, but she kept running. Night air slapped at her face, stinging her windblown cheeks.

Wet ground slid beneath her, and before she could regain her footing, she was flying through the air. Hard earth connected with her stomach. Breath fled her lungs.

Serena lay dazed, trying to untwist her limbs and stand. White stars danced in her eyes. *Air.* She needed air.

As she attempted to stand and flee, a hand clamped over her mouth, dragging her back down. Again, the breath whooshed from her lungs. She tried to slash at her captor with her dagger, but he grabbed her wrist, forcing her to toss the weapon on the cold earth.

Her back hit the ground as the hand fled her mouth, Milosh now pinning her arms above her head, leaning over her body. Hot breath fanned her face. "Stop it at once."

The deep rumble of his voice made her pause, panic crowding out courage. He looked down at her in confusion as if he couldn't place where'd seen her before, and Serena cringed under his scowl.

"If you promise to behave, I will get up."

She nodded, her face burning, suddenly aware of how close his body was to hers.

Milosh eased away, freeing her and rising to his full height. He crossed his arms, glancing her up and down. Faint recognition dawned in his eyes once more before disappearing. "Get up."

Serena's panic rose as she stood on shaky legs. She was alone—with the notorious Prince Milosh. Again. She clenched her hands, not daring to glance down to where she hoped her Marks remained covered.

Milosh motioned his head back to the camp. "You're coming back with me."

"But—" Panic tightened Serena's chest. "But I didn't do anything, and my camp is just over the hill. I cannot leave my belongings."

"You haven't done anything... yet." He leaned forward until his breath touched her face. She could not read his thoughts, could not tell if he yet recognized her. "You're coming with me."

And Serena found she had no choice but to follow, with his hand on her shoulder and her heart pounding in her throat. "Ye cannot hold me captive when I've done nothing."

"Oh, can't I?" Milosh didn't say anything else until they stood at his fire, his brown eyes penetrating hers. A wolf howled somewhere in the distance. She shifted, her face heating up under his unnerving stare.

"I know who you are," he said at last. "The wild fairy I had to toss in the castle dungeons." Milosh bent down, stirring the fire, his eyes never once leaving hers. "I can only imagine what you're doing here. And lying never works, so do not bother trying to hide why you came. I've seen the symptoms of lying too many times." He breathed a laugh. "Traitors and false friends—I've seen them all." He stopped and raised an eyebrow. "I take it you came to rescue him?"

She refused to answer. He didn't know her as Hunter's sister, and she refused to do anything but pretend innocence of any crime.

"Don't be absurd. No lass would creep through the night only to watch me while I sleep. You came for him. I know you did. I am not as much of a jack's behind as some seem to think."

Serena lifted her chin, but inside everything shook. "And if I did?"

"Then I would have to hold you as my prisoner."

"Ye already are."

Milosh laughed, but his tan face held no warmth. Taking a rope from the satchel by his feet, he began to tie her hands and feet. "I didn't think you were one to give up easily."

"I know when I've been defeated." However, deep inside she trembled.

Milosh sat back, rubbing his dark stubble on his chin, assessing her with his piercing gaze. "Tell me where your camp is and I'll get your things."

Serena glanced over her shoulder, the night swallowing the place she'd just moments before tried to sleep. "Over there about twenty paces away."

"All right." Milosh glanced her over once more, at her thin dress and windblown hair. His eyes held no lust, but still shivers racked her body. He reached down, picking up his blanket and tossed the thick fabric over her shoulders. "Sit down." And then he proceeded into the darkness.

Serena tried to regain warmth, chewing her lip. Exhaustion stole through her, her lids heavy. Where was Hunter? Was he cold, lonely, or was his mind only on what he was doing to save the lads of Sindaleer? Would he meet the Guardians? Would they help him with his mission?

Oh, she was a fool. Why had she ever thought she could do something to help him?

Sleep closed her eyes despite the cold, but before she could fully succumb, she heard Milosh's footsteps entering the camp. She heard him lead her mare next to his, glancing up as he dropped her blanket over her legs, her satchel on the ground. "Is… is everything still there?"

"Yes. I didn't take out anything." The prince lit his pipe and sat down, taking a drawl. He grimaced, the smoke trickling into the night sky. Already the darkness was beginning to lift as a pale light dawned in the east.

Her blanket lifted, and Serena's gaze snapped to her feet as Milosh reached for her foot. She drew back, kicking him in the face.

"What the h—" He grabbed his nose where she had kicked him, and roughly lifted the blanket again, grabbing her foot and yanking the dagger out. He held the weapon up and jutted out his chin as if to say, *this is what I was after—not you.*

Serena drew in a breath of the cold air, lying back down. The maids called him "a right feast for the eyes." His dark eyes almost blended with his pupils. His black

125

curls hung longer than when she'd last seen, reaching beyond his ears, different from that of the normal Sindaleer man. Handsome he may be, tempting he was not.

She turned over, remembering once when the maids spoke of guessing who would one day marry the prince. "I think we all want to marry a handsome prince so we never have to work," Ardith had said, a flirty look crossing her face. "Of course handsome Milosh will never pick any of the lasses, he's such a recluse."

"And he's a bastard. No one wants a man whose parentage isn't respectable."

"Oh, I'll never marry a prince, and still I'll be happy," Serena remembered saying softly. "I want to marry, that is all I wish, to find a man who loves me for who I am and not for what I will never be." *And even that will never happen,* she had added for only herself and herself alone, for who would marry a Marked?

14

Morning dawned bright and crisp. Serena shivered and crawled out from under the blankets, only to find that doing so with bound hands proved to be cumbersome. She was certain she looked more snake and less lass. Her eyes still weighed down with too little sleep, a pounding of drums echoing in her head.

All night, she'd lain on her back, listening to the howl of wolves and coyotes, the whistling of the wind in the treetops, and the rustle and crack of every branch. The night's events had rolled over and over in her mind and chased off any hope of sleep. Her eyes wide, she remembered only drifting once or twice.

Serena found Milosh throwing more wood on the fire, the smell of breakfast wafting from a little pot. Hunger pains stabbed her belly, reminding her that the night before she'd eaten nothing.

In the morning light, she could see that he couldn't be but a few summers older than she. Dressed in a leather jerkin over his black tunic and boots that reached his knees, he stood tall and rigid, reeking of confidence.

A confidence that disgusted Serena.

Milosh laid down the bowl and untied the ropes from her wrists before handing her a cup of broth. "If you do anything …"

Serena nodded, lifting the bowl to her mouth, the liquid burning her throat. She grimaced at the tasteless broth.

She studied the prince from beneath the brim of the cup. *How much time would pass before the medallion worked?* A shudder stole through her. *And how painful would the death be?*

If the medallion failed to work quickly, then Milosh would have time to throw it off... but mayhap... if death came in an instant...

Watching the prince out of the corner of her eye, she reached down where he had somehow failed to notice the pouch, her hand trembling. Enid knew this would happen, had somehow foreseen that Serena would be this close. Her time had come, Enid had told her.

And in a very real way, Enid's motivations were not simply pure evil, but rose from deep pain and heartache. Serena knew that motivation well, for the sorceress had turned the tables, forcing her to come face to face with her own choices.

Serena could do the deed now, find Hunter, and flee. Milosh's life would have faded in a day, and Enid would begin her revenge to take back the throne for the folk of Sindaleer.

Nay. These thoughts must wait for another time.

Who have I become?

Glancing up, her eyes drank in the sight of the sun creeping slowly over the ridgeline of trees, but darkness still hovered. "Will I ride my horse?"

Milosh glanced down at her as he fed her mare an apple, patting the creature's nose and whispering words she couldn't hear.

"Are ye going to bind me again?" she asked quietly.

"Nay, but I am taking all your belongings, and I swear if you run away you'll live to regret it." He pointed his finger at her. "You are a little hovering fairy who drifts toward me at every turn. You will ride alone and watch Hunter pay for what he did, and then I'm going to lock you up for good."

He studied her closer. "I've seen you elsewhere, after we were in jail together... nor at the village during the Ceremony." He frowned, running his fingers through his curly hair.

Serena gathered up her rolled blanket, ignoring his pondering.

"With Hunter behind the barracks!"

"Aye, perhaps ye are right," she said, her heart pounding.

"I know I am. A bloody fool I was. You aren't his lover at all... his sister." Milosh continued to mumble to himself as he cleared the camp.

Serena felt her cheeks turning pink, and she glanced down at the blanket in her hands. Milosh brushed past her and stamped out the fire, kicking dirt over the logs. They packed their horses, then saddled. Milosh's gaze strayed to hers, but she refused to acknowledge him.

The trees grew dense here. She contemplated running off, leaving Milosh to find her brother alone. She would get Hunter away from the mad prince, and perhaps they would never return to Sindaleer, leaving Enid behind like a nightmare that vanishes come morning.

But then the thoughts fled.

She would wait until they found Hunter before she tried to kill Milosh. Now was too soon, for she had not a clue where her brother was and Milosh was her only way to him.

What had she become? Was Enid's twisted Gift affecting her? Were the dreams and wishes and thoughts no longer her own?

"And ye do not want to kill him," a little voice in her head whispered. "Ye think even he, a bastard son, doesn't deserve death—not in this way."

"Shush," she quietly answered herself. "Ye are a fool to ever contemplate otherwise."

✗

Serena rode beside Milosh the first day, but his eyes never left the road. They followed the main road to the south, Serena's mind slowly growing numb.

Stuck.

She was terribly and admittedly stuck and no amount of rethinking was going to get her out of this one. Her bright idea, her sudden burst of courage, was going to get her and Hunter both killed.

Milosh may have been mocked in the village for

being only but a dummy for the king, but she knew he was no man's fool. The intensity and power of his actions and words told her so. He would not be controlled by any folk unless he willed.

Her backend ached as the afternoon sun rose high in the sky, and the captor and his maiden captive allowed their horses to slow to a walk. "How far are we going?" Her head swam and she licked her lips, craving moisture. She'd drunk a few sips of water, but the broth from that morning felt leagues away as hunger pains gnawed at her empty stomach.

Milosh glanced back, but said nothing. Serena bit her lip, and pushed her tangled hair back away from her face. She touched her heels to the horse's side, commanding the animal to keep up with Milosh.

"How far are we going on this journey?"

Milosh's hair fell around his ears, his eyes fixed on the dirt road ahead. The wind whispered through the trees by the road, and great gray clouds rolled off to the east. "All the way to the bottom."

"Ye mean to the ports in the south?"

"Yes. We shall make it in thirty days, mayhap forty."

"What about the other outlying villages? Surely ye didn't forget them and the lads ye wanted?"

"You forget," Milosh said roughly. "Hunter cannot read and therefore could not read all that was written on the maps."

"Ye are still getting more lads!" Had Clovis told her that already? She couldn't remember.

Milosh's face remained sullen with little emotion.

"My men have already gathered them as we speak. Hunter is saving less than he realizes. He can by no means save them all."

Serena couldn't hold back the disgust for this man and his black steed. Mayhap he didn't deserve death, but he surely deserved a good tongue lashing.

"Forgive me, Sire," Serena answered coldly. "To a saved lad, every rescue is a victory. Hunter wins no matter if only one lad's life is spared."

Night fell, the stars hovering like little tiny candles far off in the blanket of darkness. The Northern Mountains remained like hills in the distance, and the land flattened into rolling plains. Milosh tied her hands in front of her once more after she'd eaten and returned from her necessities.

Serena studied his face, the hard lines running down his forehead, his eyes black and unsympathetic. She was naive in the ways of men, she knew their less than honorable intentions. She had seen the evidence of their cruelty when she lived in the south where prostitutes came out even in the light of day, had known all too well the leering faces of the soldiers in the castle.

Milosh threw wood into a pile, taking out his flint and kneeling down, attempting to allow the sparks to catch. He tore a piece of rag to stuff among the wood. Still, soaked from past rains, the cloth rendered his efforts useless.

Serena's bound hands ached to work. "Let me free please. I... I can do it."

Milosh grunted. "As if you could do any better than I."

The Broken Prince

"I have more… experience."

"Ha."

"'Tis true," Serena insisted.

Milosh shook his head, continuing to watch sparks fly from his flint.

"Please. I do not wish to be cold."

Milosh cursed and whirled around, cutting her bonds and stuffing the flint into her open hands. Her wrists, chafed raw, burned as she rubbed them and attempted to get the blood flowing. Her sleeves inched up, and her breath hitched. Without glancing up at the prince, she shoved the fabric back down over her tattoos given to her by King's men.

Milosh's face held defiance as he stood over her, his arms folded. Her breathing evened—he hadn't seen. "I'm waiting."

Serena nodded, bending over the twigs and little logs. Just as with Milosh, the little flint appeared useless.

Milosh sighed and turned to his horse, muttering something under his breath about her stupidity. Serena paused, concentrating, willing the fire to burst forth before Milosh turned back around.

Her heart thudded, warmth flooding her body, racing down her arms. Her fingernails glowed orange, the palms of her hands holding a faint yellow tint.

She trembled, willing the flames to be small. Heat collided with the chilled outdoors. Smoke trickled up from the little balls of fire, rising up into the sky in gray wisps.

Serena bent down, hovering above the cold wood with her fingertips. The fire sparked, the twigs snapping

133

into a small but roaring fire.

Milosh whirled around, and Serena jumped up, balling her hands in a fist. "How did you do that?"

Serena walked over to him, placing the flint back in his hand, smiling. "I told ye … I've had more practice."

✗

Hunter halted his horse at the tip of the small mountain to admire how far he'd come. He'd journeyed for four days, his eyes fixed on the first village over the mountain he'd copied from Milosh's map.

It would take traveling over a hundred miles before he would reach the southernmost villages. His mount nickered, stepping to the side. Hunter patted his neck, leaning back in the saddle.

Silence roared in his ears. Alone. This reminded him of how he had ventured out into the wilderness to prove his manhood for the Ceremony. The heavy silence whispered around him. The prince and Bron in all its glory and shadow felt miles behind.

A rustle of a bush caught his ear.

Hunter turned, but not before an arrow sliced past his cheek, hitting a tree in front of him. His hand dove for his own bow, but a loud voice rang out in the once peaceful still. "If you favor your hand, I would not reach for your bow again."

Hunter sucked in a breath. His horse stamped beneath him. Above him a bird shot out of the trees. "Who are ye? I'm only a traveler passin' through."

"The better question might be, who are *you*?"

"I'm—I'm Hunter from near the capitol." He swung towards the shot. A round shield poked out from around a tall oak, the emblem of an eagle carved in the middle. He'd been told about that shield. "I... are ye Brunshield, head of the southern Guardians?"

A dark figure stepped out of the brush, his bow lowered. "Aye, I am. And who are you?"

"I'm..." Hunter stopped, trying to decide if he should answer for the second time. "I'm Hunter... I'm one of the lead smugglers, and I'm here to help get the lads out of the villages before the prince arrives."

Brunshield drew back the hood of his cloak, his dark face beyond tan, the hue of rich earth. "*Hunter*, lead smuggler and here to help the villages before the prince arrives. Welcome. We've been waiting for your safe arrival."

Serena awoke to her head pounding, her feet stiff and sore. Darkness covered the land like a heavy cloak. She groaned, managing to sit up. Her bonds cut her wrists, but she refused to complain.

Already Milosh had stirred the coals of the fire, and the wood crackled in the still air. Serena's hair hung limp and dirty around her head, her face covered in grime. She longed for a stream, but Milosh had never offered to let her go unless to hide among the bushes to relieve herself.

She remembered watching Milosh the night

135

before as he stared into the fire, the flames like pictures in his dark eyes. He'd been silent the whole day, not speaking even when he handed her some of the food he ate. She drank the last of her water, the hunger pains now a dull ache in her stomach. What had he been trying to prove by ignoring her?

When Serena laid down on the hard ground as fireflies flickered on and off in the dusk like candles, her eyes never wavered from the prince's face. She could see why the lasses spoke of him, but his eyes… his strength, the black hair that curled at the back of his neck, none of that captured her as his eyes did. The rich brown could turn to black in a breath, yet beyond the layers of hardness, vulnerability and pain lay.

Emotions she didn't understand. He had already proved ruthless, the rumors of what he had done to traitors of the king had been spread throughout the land.

She sighed, turning over and waiting for Milosh to sleep. In his stupor he'd forgotten to tie her hands or feet, and she didn't dare show her hands, almost afraid to breathe. If he didn't tie her…

Crickets began to fill the air with their song, and by her calculations, the second month of fall would soon be upon them. The solid ground prodded her side but she refused to move, trying to bring her breathing to normal.

Milosh, however, stayed awake far into the night. His breathing never deepened, and instead he spent much of the rest of the night tossing and turning.

Serena's eyelids grew heavy from exhaustion and waiting, and before she could stop herself, delicious sleep had consumed her.

15

*A*fter *the cold-blooded killing in the dungeons, as Milosh stood in his chambers, washing the blood of the traitor off of his hands, he gazed into the reflection piece above the water.*

Into the face of a killer.

He was no longer the innocent bastard of the hated king, but a puppet for the vile man who had forced himself onto his Mam, shaming her and other maidens like her.

Milosh's stomach twisted. The tinted water in the bowl sloshed like the contents in his stomach. Thayer was trying to create a monster out of him, and Milosh would let him think he was succeeding.

Let him think he had resigned to his fate. Let his father teach him battle tactics, to read and write, to gain allies, and become a stronger man than the monster who had created him.

Because one day Milosh's time would come, and

he would take the throne from Thayer. The cruelty done to his folk would be avenged, and if that meant playing puppet first, pulling the wool over the eyes of the man he wanted to watch bleed on the ground, then so be it.

His time was coming, and no one would stand in the way of him and the throne. He'd been weak once. He wouldn't make the same mistake twice.

A pale light hovered in the east, Milosh stirred the fire before pouring some liquid he'd been warming into a small cup. He leaned over Serena, his disobedient curls brushing his forehead. "Here."

Serena took the cup, nodding her thanks. Warm steam touched her face, clouding her vision. Fog danced through the trees, the damp soaking through her dress and cloak.

The smell of catnip mingling with mint tea brought unwanted longing for home burning in her belly. She wanted Hunter; she wanted their cottage and the Northern Mountains behind the village.

Nay, she wanted the past. Curse it all, she wanted what she could never have—freedom from fear.

Turning around, Serena sipped her tea, allowing the warmth to flow through her veins. Blood pulsed in her temples, the flames rising under her skin, fluid, wishing to be set free. And she mustn't let them.

Frustration rubbed her emotions raw. She may have missed her only chance.

Milosh saddled the horses, his rigid back towards

her.

"What do ye want with my brother if yer soldiers are beating him to the lads? What use is a simple manservant?" The words slipped between her teeth before she could catch them back.

Milosh glanced back at her. "Mayhap because the king orders me, or are you too simple minded to think of that yourself?"

"Mayhap so, but I assumed ye would be prince enough to think for yeself."

"I think girl, you bloody well keep all assumptions to yourself."

Serena quickly looked away as his eyes sparked, and it was silent a quick moment before he spoke again. "Your brother is a traitor. He thought I would be soft, that I would let him leave. He thought wrong. Hunter should have known he could never trust me."

Talk from the prince became rare following their conversation, and the two weeks drifted into mirrored sameness. After a long day's ride, they would sleep, Serena's hands and feet tied, little food in her belly. She would listen to the nighttime sounds, dreams and death and danger and Hunter filling her sleeping hours.

By the second week, she noticed that her arms became leaner, and when she stared into a stream one day to wash her face, she saw that her cheeks now sunk inward, her face tan and leathered from long rides in the sun.

Days mingled one with the other. Milosh never spoke of Hunter, never mentioned if they drew near to him, never gave her a hint of how far south they had become. He made sure they stayed as far from fellow travelers and village folk as possible, and Serena wondered if he planned on finding her brother by sheer luck.

The vast wilderness lay between them and Hunter, and in a country like Sindaleer, she knew he could be anywhere.

But one day soon stood out from the rest. Surprise filled her as he led her horse into a nearby village that she had assumed they would pass like all the rest. The village stood out of the way of the main road, smoke rising from chimneys of no more than ten or twelve thatched cottages.

A sheep village.

Black and white sheep grazed in the open pastures, young lads sitting on the edge of fences talking and watching their charges. Three men wrapped in furs to ward off the autumn chill talked together at the edge of the lodge facing the lads.

Milosh rode toward them, raising a hand in greeting, his face unreadable.

"Hello strangers." The tall man in the group raised a hand in return, bowing slightly in welcome. "How may we be of service to ye and yer lass there?"

"We wondered if a lad had passed through here mayhap a few days before us? He has short brown hair, speaks from the south. He is mayhap five and ten summers."

The man glanced at Serena and back at Milosh, his companions watching the confrontation in mutual silence.

141

"Who's asking?"

"A friend."

Hah. Serena tried to hide her distaste.

"We've had Guardians pass through. No more." He turned abruptly, but Milosh called out.

"Then we will ask no more, but do you have a place for us to stay tonight?"

"Nay, I don't think..."

"Oh, come on, Grim. Give them the old cottage by the barn—for the lass's sake," one of the other men folk spoke up. "Have some heart, mate."

Grim's eyes met Serena's, and he hesitated. "Aye, I 'spose so." His gaze went back to Milosh's. "But we answer no more questions, and be gone by morning."

✗

Night shadowed the earth once more. Serena's breathing quickened as she buried deeper underneath her blanket, her eyes peering above the scratchy fabric. Milosh as he lay under his own blanket across the fire, his black shirt blending with the darkness.

Outside, the still around them both comforted and soothed. The stone walls around them spoke of safety and sleep for mayhap this one night. Her bound hands and feet did not bother her so much.

Another long day drew to a close.

Another day that Milosh had not noticed the little pouch around her waist. *It's magic,* her mind whispered.

Or something more sinister.

Guilt pricked at her heart, needling its way in.

Killing someone had never been part of her agenda.

That evening, one of the lads from the village had brought her and Milosh a live rabbit. The boy had crept to the door of the cottage, the snow-white creature in his arms.

"Stop skulking in the shadows," Milosh had said. "Come on, boy."

The little lad's leather breaches were worn, the ends coated in mud, and he'd worn no tunic, his skin almost black from the sun. He'd offered Milosh the rabbit. "For ye," he'd said. He'd bit his lip as if nervous. "The Elders said it's a gift."

Milosh took the creature and nodded. "Thank you."

The lad had shifted from one bare foot to the other on the dirt floor.

Milosh had lifted a brow. "Well?"

"Da said yer from the north."

"And?"

"What's it like with the cities and the castle and the soldiers?" the lad had asked excitedly, the words coming out in one rush.

"Dirty," Milosh had said simply. "Go on, lad. We thank you." The lad had glanced from Milosh to Serena before dashing out the door. Milosh had looked down at the rabbit. He'd drawn his dagger from his belt, holding the blade up to the creature's neck.

Serena had watched him without speaking. He'd closed his eyes, murmuring words so low she couldn't hear. Then, with careful precision, he'd sliced the animal's fluffy neck. Blood had pooled down onto his hands and the sleeves of his tunic. "Well, I suppose we have supper."

"The words," Serena had said. "What did ye say?"

"I thanked the rabbit for giving us life." Milosh had walked over to the doorway as he began to slice open the dead rabbit.

"Ye don't..." Serena had stopped before her surprise got her in trouble.

Milosh had looked over his shoulder. "Go on. Say it. You know you want to. It surprised you, did it not? Me mourning a death?" He cursed low under his breath. "Whatever rumors went around about me, Serena, I do not enjoy senseless killing. I am not proud of what my father ordered me to do in my youth." Then, without waiting for her to respond, he'd disappeared outside.

Now, as night slipped on, Serena rolled over onto her side as she watched Milosh's breathing in the firelight, his chest moving in slow rhythm. Acid burned her throat.

She could feel the magic, the contact with the medallion against her waist sickening her. She could not understand the darkness that shadowed her heart with its touch, but nonetheless, the darkness remained, taunting her. Enid wanted a life, and this gold piece would take one.

Milosh's face glowed in the firelight separating the two of them. The warm flames flickered, casting shadows around the walls. He stirred, murmuring under his breath.

He didn't trust her. She didn't trust him.

Every day they drew closer to Hunter. Any day her brother may appear over the ridgeline.

Serena bit her lip. The smell of the pine from his clothing mingled with the woodsmoke in the air.

Now. Do it now.

Her hand slipped in the pouch around her waist, the cold seeping through her skin. The force pulled at her, stronger than her will to stop it.

Kill him. Kill him.

She rose to her feet. Her heartbeat hammered in her chest. Thrumb. Thrumb. White vapors from the cold drifted into the air with every breath she took.

"Destiny forgive me," Serena murmured. Like the rabbit had to die so they could eat, Milosh had to die so Hunter could have life. Firelight flickered off Milosh's sleeping form curled under his blanket. She stretched out her arm, bending down. "May yer death not pain ye."

The line to the throne would end here.

"Nay!"

Every fiber of her being froze. Her skin glowed a dangerous orange. Milosh began to thrash, his eyes still closed. She let out a breath—a dream.

He was only dreaming. But he would wake up the entire village with his yells.

A hand clamped around her wrist.

Serena's heart dropped to her cold toes. She tried to wrench from his grasp, but Milosh held on fast. Her hand grew numb.

"I let you go this night and now you are trying to kill me." He drew a dagger from his belt. Serena tried to step back, but the sharp tip made a tiny slit on her neck.

145

She cried out, trying to stop the blade from slitting her throat. Her legs swayed, her tired feet planted to the ground. "Sire," she panted. "Ye are dreaming. Stop!"

Milosh peered at her through glazed eyes. "Ye have taken my mam from me, and now ye wish to kill me! Why did ye prolong the agony?" He began to weep, tears streaming down his face like a small child.

Serena's heart shook in her chest. The prince was returning back to the southern dialect of his birthplace. Without taking her eyes off him, she slipped the medallion back in its pouch.

Milosh held up the other hand, the blade never wavering from her neck. "Look at my fingers!" he yelled.

Serena shook, trying to nod, trying to see his hand in the darkness. The fingers were black and blue, the knuckles cracked. She'd seen the wounds before, guessing that he'd received them in training, an error of some sort.

"I hate ye," Milosh said. "I hate what ye have done to me, and I will forever hate ye. See this? Everyday I try to find ways to rebel, to show that ye do not control me." He shoved up his sleeve, revealing the tattoo Serena had only caught a glimpse of before.

The Serpent of Death. Serena shuddered at the sight of the mark in the firelight. The blade nicked more of her skin.

The creature held the fear of all of Sindaleer, especially those who lived by the Cimmerian Forest. One bite and the victim would be dead within a day, a pain like no other causing him to suffer during all of his last hours.

"I did this," Milosh all but shouted. "I did this because of you. I am bloody feared and despised because of you. I am a bastard! No one accepts me because you raped Mam!"

Serena cried out as her blood ran faster, trying to move her hands. She made ready to burn him, to wake him and let him see reason. She raised her hand, but he shoved her away with his free one. "Nay! Do not touch me!"

"Wake up, sire. Please! Wake up!" Smoke drifted from her fingertips.

Milosh studied her face. The glazed look slid from his eyes. "Serena?" The dagger wavered.

"Aye, sire."

The tears on Milosh's face had begun to dry. He wiped them away with the back of a dirty hand. "Serena?"

"Aye."

The dagger dropped to the floor. Serena staggered backward.

"I... I was bloody dreaming." The words came out stiff and awkward.

Serena breathed a shaky laugh. "Aye." She stepped further back, glancing down. Her sleeves had somehow rolled up past her wrists. She hurried to fix them.

Reaching out to touch the prick on her neck, Serena only felt dried blood. The wound would be scabbed by morning.

She drew in an unsteady breath, pulling the

147

blanket around her shoulders as she half laid, half flopped to the ground, a shudder snaking through her body.

Milosh still sat in the cold, staring into the flames of the fire. As if in a trance, he stirred the logs with a stick, watching red hot ashes fall to the side. Enid had been wrong back at the day in the cottage when she spoke of King Thayer treating Milosh like a beloved son.

Nay, Milosh was simply a puppet for the king. Mayhap Milosh did naught to cease being such, but he was a puppet all the same. He had been taken away from his village, promised power if only he did the king's will. What lad would not have relented at last?

Milosh gazed over at her, breaking her thoughts away from her. Something warm stirred in Serena's heart. Empathy, mayhap. Because she had a habit of feeling sorry for the outcasts in this world.

And curse it all, she felt compassion.

16

Milosh rode behind today, saying he needed to keep a good eye on her. In fact, his only words had been that. He'd said nothing since.

Serena guessed that she alone knew the things he'd voiced last night, and in a peculiar sense she understood him. Folks remained none too forgiving in Sindaleer and they never forgot past deeds—even if they were the deeds of the parents.

Aye, Serena knew that all too well.

And Milosh's father had done terrible things his first year as king. He and the soldiers had defiled the women folk, bringing shame upon their households. Milosh had been one of those bastard babies and he too, though he did not bear The Mark as she did, had been brought low.

However, his anger, no matter how understandable, could not be deemed just. Lads would die if Thayer, as rumors spoke, raged war on another country. They would be nothing more than pawns under Milosh's control with little choice but to obey.

Her irritation flared higher with the remembrance that he hadn't let them conclude the Ceremony, that widows were now without sons, and that he could not be brave enough to stand up against his father.

Folk deemed it a great honor to have been blessed by the elders as a man, but Thayer took lads from their home before they could have that chance. Milosh may despise his King Thayer, but by all appearances, he would not risk his father's ire by disobeying his orders.

Serena turned in the saddle, throwing out caution along with her frustration, and dared a question that came out more flippant than she intended. "Do ye always have loud dreams?"

Milosh's face hardened, and he stared straight past her.

Serena tried again, angry enough to coax him to wrath. "Ye spoke of many things last night. Do ye remember?"

Milosh's jaw flexed. He urged his horse faster, passing her on the road.

In the name of all things good. "Ye spoke of quite a lot."

"And you'd do well to forget it."

"Aye, but I do not think that is possible."

"Speaking of it will mean an arrow between your eyes."

Ye arrogant prince! "Father like son—isn't that how the saying goes? Are ye going to be like yer father?"

"Nay!" Milosh's hand reached for his bow, pulling back the string. An arrow zinged beyond Serena's face, the tip smiting her cheek. She gasped, her heartbeat pounding faster than horse's hooves at full gallop. Blood trickled down her face.

Her eyes grew wide, tears smarting her eyes from the smarting of the little wound by her eye.

So this was how it would be. Apparently Milosh's heart had grown as cold as his mind, last night's unwitting confessions hardening his vulnerability. He would indeed kill her if the fancy arose. She journeyed with a man who feared becoming a monster but everyday grew closer and closer to being exactly that.

She raised her eyes to Milosh's face. His skin had taken on a deathly pallor, his eyes wide with shock. "I—I..." He lowered the bow, hands trembling.

He leaned forward, his hands shaking. Serena thought he might be crying, but moments later he raised his head, his eyes dark with anger. "I will *never* be my father."

17

The mountain road where Serena and Milosh traveled, grew level the further south their horses carried them. Warmer winds surrounded her, and above her head the trees creaked.

Serena used to think the small creaks were small kittens calling for help, stuck in the branches. She recalled once telling Da so.

"Don't be so easily fooled," she remembered him saying. "Mayhap one day ye'll learn to actually see life as it is. Not everything is as it first appears. Learn that quickly little lass."

Serena gazed up at the massive trunks, their branches wavering in the gathering breeze. Da had never approved of her storytelling, of her wish-making, of the legends she and Hunter would whisper to each other during the long winter evenings.

She glanced back at Milosh, his hard eyes staring through her.

Mayhap, her Da had been right. Mayhap she would never see reality.

Earlier they had passed through a small town where Milosh had bought fresh provisions, including freshly baked bread. Together, they had devoured half a loaf as they sat in the sunshine on a log inside the town square.

An old peddler had hobbled by with a tiny lad at his wrinkled hand. The man had held a stick, stones hanging off on leather thongs. "Necklace for the pretty lass?" he'd rasped.

Milosh had shaken his head. "Not today, old man."

"Are ye sure, my Lord?" the man had insisted. His lad wiped his runny nose with the back of his hand. "Money goes for me lad, so he can eat a mite tonight?"

Milosh had shaken his head again.

"Nothing for yer lass? To show her yer love?"

The lad had watched Milosh and Serena with droopy eyes, his feet bare, and his tunic barely covering his skinny legs.

"No money but—" Milosh had hesitated, his gaze darting to the lad. He'd picked up the remainder of the bread, and shoved it at the peddler. "Take it."

"Thank ye!" The lad's eyes had lit up, and he'd grabbed it, taking a bite, crumbs clinging to his chin.

"A necklace then?" The peddler had lifted one off the rack, a blue stone hanging from the thin thong. He'd lifted the jewel over Serena's head, smiling. "Ye make a lovely couple. Ye shall have beautiful lads and lasses one day."

Then, without another word, he and the lad had disappeared into the crowd.

Serena's face had lit up in embarrassment as the two walked away, but in that moment, she couldn't help but think—somewhere, under that rough exterior, the prince of Sindaleer really did have a heart.

✗

"Halt! In the name of the Mountain men, halt!"

Serena's mare danced to the side, trying to turn off the path. She cried out as she began to slide, toppling to the ground. Her breath whooshed from her lungs as she hit the ground. Hard.

Serena gasped, holding her stomach. Air. She needed air.

Strong hands reached out to grab her, yanking her to her feet. Milosh let out a yell, cursing a fire storm of words as they pulled him off his horse. "Curse the Marked! What in the name of Thayer are you doing?"

Serena attempted to turn to face her captor, but he pushed her forward beyond the road and through some trees to stand beside Milosh. He glanced over at her and back at their captors, his face gray with anger.

Serena followed his gaze. Before them stood seven men, their faces covered up to their eyes with brown cloth. They wore stained deerskin clothing, fur vests over their dirty and torn shirts. Their fur-lined moccasins went almost beyond their knees, but these too had seen many winters.

Mountain men. Any folk from Sindaleer that

were right in the mind, knew a Mountain Man when he or she saw one. These folk acted as though the mountains were their lands and only their lands, forcing the travelers to pay heavy fees to cross over the border and down to the other side. If you couldn't pay, death was yours.

"What wrongs have we committed?" Milosh demanded. "We only wish to pass over the mountain." He tried to stand, but the youngest of the men, who looked to be no more than five and ten summers, pushed him back down.

"Oi! And who are ye to talk, ye no good passerby? We live on these mountains! Ye have no say in what we do."

"Calm it, Breck." The oldest of the men glared at Milosh as he held out his spear to the prince's throat. "These folks may be of some use to us."

The other men snickered, and Milosh shot them a glare that could have burned if he'd had the gifting for it. "You are all touched in the head. I'm Milosh, son of Thayer! I deserve some respect!"

"Ye have relations with the king!" Breck exclaimed, turning to his father. "Da, this lad says he's close with the king."

"Aye, Brun," another man called out, pushing the point of his spear near Milosh's shoulder. "This lad here says he's a prince."

Brun eyed the two captives. "An' who would believe it? Almost too good to be true." He grabbed Serena's chin and glared down at her, his breath reeking of stale smoke from his pipe. She trembled, trying to turn her head away from him.

Beside her, Milosh stiffened.

"Aye," Brun said. He ran a hand down her cheek. "'Tis right. 'Tis too good ta be true, that it 'tis." He pushed Serena's head back further, running a hand along her hair. She tried to bite him, but he sprung back in time. She shuddered.

"Let go of her," Milosh growled. Once more he tried to stand, but Breck ran around where the man held a spear to his chest.

"Kill 'im now and let's 'ave the lass."

Brun stepped back. "Shet up, Breck. We need to see if this son of a rat is lyin'. If he is the prince we may get a bit of somethin' for 'em. Then ye can have the lass!"

Breck cursed. "Ye mean I 'ave to be the one to go find?"

"Aye. Whether he's the son of the high and cursed Thayer or not, ye can still have the lass. Hades, mayhap we can all have a turn. Jest find out, Breck."

Breck grabbed the bow he left leaning against an oak. "Mean it?"

"She's all yers."

Serena shivered, her teeth chattering together, scraping across her lip. If Breck put his hands on her, she would blow him sky high, and he would come back only ash.

A muscle in Milosh's jaw ticked. His eyes remained steely, unflinching. Surprise coursed through her. Milosh shouldn't care whether or not someone laid hands on her. He had proved unfeeling hours before.

But deep down, a part of her spirit couldn't help

but trust him. He'd shown her honor and respect in ways his father never had.

Muttering, Breck slung the full quiver of arrows around his back, bounding off into the woods. Brun made sure the captives' hands were bound properly, causing Milosh to flinch as he tied the ropes tighter.

Serena kept her mouth shut as her bonds dug into her wrists, but she longed to have them free so she might use her Gift. If only her hands weren't tied behind her back, her fingers curled towards her back.

Two men strode up to the two captives, and dragged Serena and Milosh back through the woods, the others leading the horses. Serena's feet slid in the mud as the big mountain man forced her to keep up with his long strides.

Serena wondered where they were taking them. Mountain Men often housed themselves away in the caves, deep in the tunnels that no folk could find. Their skills at staying hidden remained uncanny, and she'd heard that the guardians often tried to learn their ways.

Serena dreaded the thought of entering their domain, for if she and Milosh did, they might never see the light of day. Tales were told at how these

Trees filled almost every space of her vision, nothing but ugly trunks. Wind whipped through the mountain pass. Summer and sunshine felt far away.

The captors forced the two to walk along a steep ridgeline. Far below them, a bed of rocks and a small stream lay. Serena shuddered, trying to peer below her as her captor shoved her along. Wind whistled between sharp rocks lining the side of the cliff.

And, despite their captivity, a tiny part of her heart sang.

Hunter.

He would get there to the far south... and mayhap, in the end, the lads would escape. Then her journey would not be in vain.

✗

Milosh tried to catch Serena's gaze. He heard her heavy breathing,and her feet dragged along the rocky ground. He knew what stories surrounded these hardened Mountain Men and should have tried to go on a different road on the lower side of the mountain. He cursed.

Now he and Serena were captured, and these men were likely to kill him and take Serena. He ground his teeth, his jaw aching. While he'd convinced himself that she seemed cursed to follow him, a maddening lass that had gotten under his skin, he couldn't shake her away from his mind into the long hours of night.

Let the Mountain Men try and touch Serena. They'd regret the day they had been born. He'd show them hell.

The spear of Milosh's captor prodded his back, the end beginning to dig through his cloak and jerkin. He winced, but his face remained stone.

He contemplated jumping down over the side of the cliff, but that would mean certain death. If the fall didn't break every bone in his body, the rocks surely would and—

Before he could catch himself, Milosh found

himself flying forward. The spear dug into his shoulder blade, causing him to fall even further. His feet tried to find something sturdy.

Little pebbles and hard ground met him. His arms flailed behind him, useless as a Marked when Thayer's soldiers were on his tail.

He hit the earth, his jaw meeting a rock. Pain forced the breath from his lungs.

Someone yelled out his name. Serena.

Warm liquid trickled down his chin, and he fought hard to keep from gagging on the blood. His tooth had bit into his lower lip, biting off a chunk.

"Oi!" Brun grabbed Milosh's shoulders and hauled him up, spitting in his face. "Ye tipsy, brainless mountain goat!" He held onto the hood of Milosh's cape, forcing him dangerously close to the cliff's edge. Milosh glanced back, trying to mask his fear.

"I should drop ye over the edge right now. I 'ave no use for ye, and I'm sure if ye really do have the king's blood in ye, t'would make no nevermind. The king hates his son anyway."

Milosh wanted to kick the man, but he feared falling over the edge. Inside he yelled oaths, wanting to deny all the accusations. Even if they were all but true.

"Not goin' to say anything, pretty lad?" The man spit in Milosh's face again, causing saliva to mix with the blood draining from Milosh's lip. Then his captor drew back, slamming his fist into Milosh's face.

18

"Milosh!" Serena's body remained still with fear. He teetered on the side of the rocks, his face white. He fell back to his knees, less than a pace from his death. Blood dribbled out of the side of his mouth.

Serena lurched free from the mountain man behind her, her tied hands leaving her unbalanced. "Let him go!"

The Mountain Man pushed Milosh closer to the edge. "He mean somethin' to ye?" His eyes darkened. Serena's guard ran forward and prodded her with his spear, but Serena paid him no heed.

The cold wind bit at her cheeks, blowing the hood of her cape off her head, seeping through her matted brown hair.

Brun laughed as if in jest, but the sound made her shudder. "Want to live, prince?"

Milosh said nothing, his eyes flashing with the hatred that had scared Serena many times. Brun started laughing and pushed Milosh at Serena, knocking her and the prince to the ground.

Her captor threw his hands up at the men. "I see they need lessons in how to take jokes, aye, men?"

His comrades joined in on the laughter, and Serena's stomach churned acid. Beside her Milosh lay on the ground, his eyes closed, his head resting on her legs. She struggled to sit, nudging him with her shoulder.

"Milosh?" At her voice, he stirred, mumbling something. "Get up."

The Mountain Men had begun talking among themselves, pointing at the trees and arguing. One brought out a jug of ale. The mood had shifted from light-hearted to angry. Serena wondered if they would get into a fight or drink themselves full until they only staggered around causing trouble.

The ground sunk like ice through Serena's cape. She shivered and nudged Milosh again. *Be alright. Please, be alright.*

His eyelids fluttered slightly, and her heart pounded. Streaks of dirt coated his cheeks, and a purple bruise was slowly forming around his eye.

She carefully brushed soft strands of dark hair away from his forehead. His eyes fluttered again and then opened, meeting hers.

Capturing her, holding her there like she was under a spell she couldn't escape.

Then she realized her hand was still resting on his face, his skin hot under her touch. She slid away like he was a fire, consuming her.

Milosh sat up, rubbing his head.

"Are ye alright?" Serena whispered.

He blinked, his eyes still glazed with confusion. "Aye, I think so."

The Mountain Men appeared to have no concern for their captives. They passed the jug of ale around, laughing and joking among themselves. Serena and Milosh huddled on the frosty ground, fatigue ruling sound thought.

Milosh's intent gaze warmed her to the core. They sat with their shoulders touching, his body heat seeping through her. He'd no princely stature about him now, dried blood crusting his beard and lip, a gash about his eye still oozing liquid.

The man who had shot the arrow was, for but a moment, a shadow of the past.

But ye can't forget the past, Serena, she reminded herself. *The past doesn't lie. He's going to take yer brother from ye.*

And yet, here and now, no barrier stood between them. This night, they were equals, both captives, both in need of the other in order to survive.

Brun held up the bottle to Milosh, then laughed. "To the prince of Sindaleer's health!"

The Mountain Men drank heartily. Cold rain like little needle points began to spread itself across the mountain. The water sprayed on Serena like mist from a waterfall, clinging to her eyelashes. When she pressed her fingertips to her cheek, her skin remained unfeeling.

She leaned against the rough bark of a tree,

pulling her knees up to her chest, aware that her and Milosh's thighs and shoulders still touched, his hair brushing her cheek. She shivered, and he stirred beside her.

"Quit your endless rattling," he said, but his tone sounded soft to her ears. He gave a deeper sigh, one of surrender. "Come here."

Serena stopped, her lips cold. She touched her cheek where the arrow had grazed. "Nay."

"We're both going to die of your stubbornness. Come here."

Serena paused. *He's dangerous,* her conscience reminded her. *But now we're both captive,* she reasoned back. *I need him to survive.*

Nay, her conscience reprimanded her again. *Ye don't need him to live. Don't forget Hunter. What is he going to do to Hunter?*

The temptation for warmth rattled her exhausted mind.

Finally, she found she could do nothing but give in.

He managed to wrap her in his cape. Together, they leaned against the giant oak, its branches waving high above them. Rain fell in a steady mist, burning her with drops that pinged off her skin like ice.

Wisps of Milosh's warmth soothed her. The Mountain Men built a roaring fire, and her eyes grew mesmerized by the gold and orange flames in the dying light of day. And, with a sigh of resignation, she leaned against Milosh's firm shoulders. He smelled of woodsmoke and wind and that blasted pipe he tried to smoke… like home, like Bron.

He's doing this to stay warm, but she pushed the thought away. The night of his dream drifted into her memory, his terrified face, and that moment when she saw more lad than demon... more than simply another version of his father.

Her eyes began to drift close, the dampness of his jerkin resting against her cheek. Mayhap Enid would leave Hunter alone if both she and Milosh died. All would be settled, and Hunter could live a life without fear for her safety.

"We're going to escape," Milosh whispered, his warm breath fanning her face. "They're becoming too drunk to see straight."

Serena gave a low laugh. "They have bows."

Milosh didn't reply at first as he watched the men laugh and jest around the warm fire. "You shall go first."

Serena turned around, their noses almost touching. She searched his face, but saw nothing to betray him. His eyes remained stony rocks. "They'll kill ye if I go first."

As if suddenly realizing how close they were, Serena almost sitting on his lap, Milosh drew back, his gaze locked with hers. He opened his mouth as if to speak, but then jumped up. "Oi!"

Serena glanced over her shoulder.

"Run! Serena, run!"

She whirled around. Milosh had somehow managed to throw his tied arms in front, smashing his fists into the face of Brun.

Serena's heart rammed against her breastbone.

Free. I need to get free.

She couldn't move her hands, and she didn't dare try her Gift with her hands tied.

Milosh let out a war cry. He grabbed one of the spears from the Mountain Men, stabbing one in the chest. Crimson flowed on the wet ground. "For the love of my mum, run, Serena!"

One of the Mountain Men barreled toward her, yelling oaths. He drew back an arrow. Serena screamed as it tore by her, ripping the cape around her shoulders.

She took off running, her tied hands sending her off balance. She tripped on a root and almost went sprawling onto the ground. She regained her balance, hearing Milosh shout again.

Nay! She would not leave him to fight alone!

She turned around and heard an arrow whiz by her head, but this time it came not for her but for her captor. The arrow sank into the shoulder of the big Mountain Man. He flew off balance, yelling and cursing as he held his arm. As he tried to rise, another arrow pierced his other shoulder.

Serena looked through the mist and drizzling rain. Her heart threatened to jump out of her chest. Another arrow missed its mark on Brun.

This had the attention of the Mountain Men now. They forgot Milosh, shoving him toward the cliff bank and grabbing for their spears and bows.

Serena whirled around towards the direction of the arrows. Cool air brushed past her legs as the wind picked up. She heard a zing and another arrow landing in the tree by her shoulder. Gasping, she jumped out of the way. Turning on her heels, she dashed back through the dusky woods, hoping beyond hope that the archers were friendly.

Her feet seemed to hardly touch the ground as she dashed over a log, skidding on wet leaves. She slid down the other side of the hill, briars tearing at her skin and clothes, falling away from the Mountain Men, away from the cliff. Away from Milosh.

Quiet roared around her. The trees became a blur of brown as she ran, her feet kicking dirt clods. Serena turned, looking over her shoulder. No folk followed.

A hand clamped over her mouth, and someone dragged her down on the ground. She tried to kick her captor in the shins but missed. Her head spun and black dots formed in her vision.

 Air. She needed air.

With one last effort she drew back, kicking him in the groin. He groaned, pushing her against his chest, her face turned away from him.

"Greetings, Sunshine."

She whirled around to face her attacker. "Elston? What in the name of Destiny are ye doing here?"

Elston, his brown hair falling over his shoulders, a shadow of a beard on his smiling face. Relief loosened the tension in her shoulders.

"Ah," he said. "But the question I have for you is, what are *you* doing here?" He winked. "Mountain Men are not known for their romance, so surely you didn't fall for one of them? I tried romancin' one of their lasses' once—too hairy."

"Oh, leave yer jesting for later. Why are ye

here?"

Elston took her arm, leading her back whence she'd come. "Ya left me in good hands, and the Guardians sent me to the south to join up here, and what do ya know, I get to save you and your man. We heard from some folk that the Mountain men were causing trouble, but we didn't realize they were taking folk prisoner."

"Until now."

Serena ignored the questions in Elston's eyes as they climbed the hill, her lungs aching from cold. Dusk fell. Her eyes caught sight of Milosh speaking with one of the guardians. The Mountain Men were nowhere in sight.

"Serena."

She glanced up into Elston's concerned face as he reached out, his warm hand on her arm. "What are you doing with the prince?"

Serena swallowed, glancing ahead to their rescuers in dark cloaks. Milosh continued to talk with the five of the Guardians, his form now straight and sure. He bore the look of a man in control, like the prince that he was. When his gaze met hers, she turned away.

"Serena."

"Elston, he... my brother... I'm his prisoner because I went after my brother," she finished.

"Has he hurt you then?" Elston's tone dipped to threatening.

"Nay!" Serena glanced over her shoulder. Milosh's intent regard caused her stomach to twist. "There's no time to explain."

Elston followed her gaze to Milosh. "Then does

he know about—"

She shook her head, pulling the loops of her sleeves more firmly around her thumbs. "Nay. He doesn't."

Elston raised his eyebrows, taking a draw from his pipe, saying nothing, his brows furrowed.

"I'm hoping I can save my brother by being Milosh's prisoner, that I can stop something terrible from happening."

"I'm not letting you go with him alone, and I'm not letting you be his prisoner."

"I don't think ye have much say in it," Serena said, ignoring his frown and hurrying over to the fire. They would have to talk later. There was no time to explain the last weeks, Enid, the medallion... the complication of it all set her head in a spin.

The warmth of the fire began to seep through her skin, thawing her frozen fingertips, drying the damp in her hair. A strong body brushed up beside hers.

Milosh crouched down, holding his chapped hands out toward the fire. He glanced over at her, his dark eyes seemingly able to probe into her thoughts. The blood had dried on his face, and the wounds reminded her that he was a prince second, but a born and bred warrior of Sindaleer above all else.

Confusion and questions pricked her conscience, but she forced them away, choosing to see the injury as proof of the little bit of chivalry he possessed.

Right.

"The Guardians are leaving now," Milosh said, breaking her thoughts, his gaze straying to Elston who studied them from his position under the shadows of a giant pine. "But they're providing us with one horse and some food and water. They drove the Mountain Men down towards the valley, capturing some of them. We should be fine."

"We can't take shelter with the Guardians?"

Milosh shook his head, but Serena could see the anger lit in his eyes. Serena already knew without asking. Milosh was unwanted. The Guardians did their duty to rescue him, but that was as far as their generosity went.

"Your fool brother will have all the lads out by the time we get there," Milosh muttered.

"He'd do whatever it takes to rescue those lads," Serena whispered. "I'm proud of him."

She stayed curled by the fire as the shadows grew, warming herself beside the stoic Milosh. Elston had left with the Guardians without a word, promising to come back.

An awkwardness lingered around them.

For one, aching moment, they had been the same., and yet, now she realized that nothing had changed.

Ages must have passed as Milosh began to pace back and forth from the fire. "Where are those fool Guardians?" he asked her irritably. "We freeze in the cold and are entirely at their mercy."

Serena ignored his cursing and muttering. "Thank ye." May as well come out with it.

"What did you say?"

"Thank ye," Serena murmured, studying the dried blood around one of his eyes and cheek. He would need the wound cleaned once the Guardians came with water.

"For what?"

"For saving me." Serena looked at her hands, red from the warmth of the fire and covered in dirt and grime, red scratches from the thorns visible on her palms.

I don't understand ye. Ye cannot make up yer mind who ye want to be.

Milosh said nothing, and Serena dared to look into his face. The hard lines around his eyes softened, and his jaw flexed. "I'm not a monster, Serena." He said the words carefully, as if he was trying to convince himself more than her.

Serena bit her lip. "I know." And she did, really. For each person has both light and darkness, evil and good, but it is up to us who will win.

Milosh had yet to make his choice.

He crouched down, his shoulder brushing hers, a little stick twirling absentmindedly between his fingers. "Sometimes I feel that I am... The darkness hovers in the back of my mind, at times choking me… My father—" He cursed.

"It doesn't have to be this way," Serena whispered. "Ye can choose who ye are..."

Milosh stiffened. "I have my orders."

"Sometimes orders are meant to be broken... Sometimes they can't be obeyed because they're wrong."

Milosh turned his face towards her, his breath fanning her face. Her skin tingled with his nearness, but she couldn't bring herself to gaze up in his face. "You are no longer my prisoner—"

The words came out so quietly Serena could've sworn she'd imagined them. Horse's hooves pounded against the hard dirt ground. Milosh jumped up, the conversation evaporating into the air as quickly as it had come.

You are no longer my prisoner.

She must have dreamed it. Serena licked her lips, her body trembling.

You are no longer my prisoner.

Elston appeared over the ridge, his eyes twinkling, holding the lead ropes of three horses. "Hullo, folks!"

"Two horses?" Milosh asked. "Guardians said I only got one."

"Aye, that you do, but I'm taking a little trip with ya, you see. I've been hankering to go further down south, and you shall be my travel companions."

Milosh clenched his fists, darts of anger flinging from him. Serena knew he couldn't say no, not after he'd brought them provisions and a horse. "Fine."

Elston winked at Serena and bowed his head. "I am at your service and will always be."

"Thank *you*," Milosh muttered.

"Ah, but I see you are full of yourself." Elston wagged a finger at the prince mockingly, throwing a wink at Serena. "For I was speaking to the lady. Hello, Springtime!"

19

"Where are you from?" Milosh asked Elston, stirring the fire.

Serena had taken the water pouch from Elston and carefully begun cleaning Milosh's wound, since his eye was now rimmed with red and purple bruises. The prince flinched as the water ran down his face.

"Here and there," Elston said, his gaze fixed on Serena as if determined to solve the mystery of why Serena and Milosh traveled together. "Most places can't keep me amused for very long. I need a little excitement in my life... There was this one time I got in a fight with a bear the size of a small cottage..."

Serena ripped a bit of her old cloak, only half-listening to Elston's tall tale as she dabbed at Milosh's wound. He flinched again. "Don't move," Serena said in an undertone.

172

"—And to be honest I was really only doing it for the lass," Elston continued his story. "But you know how it goes."

Milosh grunted in reply.

As carefully as she could, she began dabbing a bit harder, but found the blood refused to come away from the prince's skin. Milosh kept turning his face, making the angle difficult for her. She lightly rested her hand on his face, turning him to face her. Milosh raised his gaze to Serena.

Serena bit her lip, dropping her hand away. She concentrated on the wound, not meeting his gaze. Her cheeks warmed.

"Thank you."

Thank you. The words were said so silently Serena wondered if her imagination had conjured the words. She lay down the rag, her hands trembling. Milosh broke his gaze, turning to Elston

She was supposed to kill him and yet... She wanted to run, flee, get far away from him. He was out of his senses, unwilling to defy his father. But he had taken the Mountain Mens' blows so she could abandon him.

Why? Why did he do this to her?

"What made you want to travel now?" Milosh was asking Elston, lighting his own pipe and taking a hesitant drawl.

Elston raised his eyebrows. "There is a pretty lass along—surely I would not refuse an opportunity to accompany her, eh, Springtime?"

Serena glanced at her hands, her face warming.

"Serena and I are old friends," Elston continued,

his eyes challenging. "I would never hesitate to protect her."

"I am sure you would not." Milosh rose, not looking at Serena, his eyes remaining on his rival. "The air is turning chilly, and I'm going to collect firewood. But I won't be far, so I would advise you to not try anything that would be less than chivalrous." With this final warning, he disappeared into the forest.

"A prince collecting firewood? I commend you," Elston spoke sarcastically to the prince's back.

"Aye, ye are a troublesome man," Serena murmured to him. "Milosh will never warm up to ye if ye continue to hound him."

"Aye, and I do not know if I care." He glanced sideways at her, grinning. "Do you care, Springtime?"

Serena glanced down at her dirty hands, not sure how to answer. "I know that Milosh has a temper I would not want to risk."

"So he *has* hurt you."

"Nay—nay, not in any way that ye are thinking." Serena's voice lowered. "I came to help my brother from Milosh's wrath, but he intercepted me, and now I am his captive. Nothing more. We are simply enemies forced to each other's company."

But the words fell unconvinced from her tongue. *You are no longer my prisoner.* The air around them had changed, but to what, she knew not.

Elston leaned forwards so that only she could hear if Milosh stood nearby. "I was not lying to Milosh, Serena. I came because of you. I am going to get you free, and we can find Hunter together."

Serena's mind raced to the medallion, her hand going to the pouch at her side. She could tell him, here and now. Elston could help her, she could trust him. "Nay. Ye can't, Elston. That won't solve the problems. There, there is more. Milosh—he has been judged wrongly by our folk..."

"Really?" Elston's eyebrows rose as if he'd heard her thoughts. "So, if I tell a story right now using my Gifts and the prince walks up on me, all will be well?"

"Well—"

Elston's eyes began to dance with humor. "Because I told a tale without using my Gifts, but what if I tell a story, one about snow and a storm and the dragon that destroys all that is evil? What if snowflakes suddenly began to fall and a dragon started flying through the sky?"

"Nay, nay." Serena breathed a laugh. "Ye will get us both in trouble."

Elston rolled his eyes. "Once upon a time, Milosh son of a bi—"

As Milosh's name rested on Elston's tongue, the prince suddenly came out of the brush, holding several little logs in his arms. He placed one in the fire, kicking away some others that had fallen, blackened, to the ground.

His black hair curled around the nape of his neck, the cuts on his face giving him that rugged appearance all the maidens spoke of.

Oh, Milosh.

I can't do what I've been commanded.

✗

Fire illuminated the dusk of the forest, the cracking of the logs breaking the silence of the cold night. Stars like crystals blinked overhead. Enid stood at the edge of the fire, her arms crossed to ward off the chill.

A whistle echoed behind her. Enid reached for the dagger at her side as a figure stepped out from between the tall pines. "You are not very confident of your Gifts, are you?" he said with a smirk. He drew back his black hood, revealing dark hair that hung about his shoulders.

"And neither are you, Tirich," Enid retorted, nodding to the spear in his gloved hand.

"But I am young and still learning. You are the one supposed to be helping the Knights build an empire and rebellion. It pains me to see our advisor afraid."

"Stop the jesting." Enid strode over to Tirich, glaring up at him. A full beard covered his face, hiding his youthful appearance and the lad she'd once known. "You know you only want me because I taught you everything you know. But you have far surpassed me in dark magic and giftings."

The young knight shrugged his broad shoulders. "Mayhap." He edged closer to the fire, warming his hands over the orange flames. "But I did not come to talk about who is better. Is the prince dead? That's why I've come."

"The girl has yet to do it."

Tirich cursed. "Why didn't you do the deed yourself? Afraid? We're wasting time waiting on her and your need for revenge." He tsked. "This obsession is not healthy."

Enid absently ran her hand over her blade. "Nay!" She began to pace. "You don't understand, do you? My power is weakening. I'm dying, Tirich. If I inflicted Milosh's death as I wanted, if I used my powers to break into the castle one more time, I would die."

"At least your death would be one of a hero. Instead, you hide in the shadows, waiting for an urchin to do your dirty work."

Enid's eyes flashed. "Stupid, Tirich. You are stupid to talk so. The medallion I gave Serena is cursed. If she fails to do what I asked, it will kill her. I have long wanted to see Thayer's kingdom slip from his grasp. I will sit on his throne, and if that means waiting on Serena, then so be it."

"You on the throne?" Tirich smirked. He lit his pipe, taking a long drawl. "Isn't that my job?"

"With me as your advisor," Enid said. "So shut up, young one. I've long waited for this glory, so let me be. Your time will come. For now, let me do my part as I wish. Milosh will die, and by my hand. Soon. Thayer's rule is ending, and we will claim the throne. Together."

Tirich waved a finger in front of her face. "Fine, but you have one week. The Knights' power is growing, and they are restless, ready to strike. You have one week or not at all."

✗

Serena's arms rested around Milosh's waist as they rode, his nearness unnerving. At first she remained rigid, and Milosh's own back was stiff and straight, as always the regal prince. His woodsy scent and the smell of trees and wet leaves soothed her, but her resolve to not put her hands around his waist, only broke as they descended downhill. Her body jolted as the horse lumbered downward, and she was forced to grab Milosh's cape.

Over the last several weeks, Serena learned many things on her trip back to the southern lands, the first of which was this: Traveling with Elston and Milosh was no easy task. While she knew Milosh often refused to speak for long periods of time, remaining gruff and sullen, his mood around Elston only worsened, who rattled off story after story just to rile the prince.

But thank Destiny, he never used his Gift.

Serena sensed tension and distrust between the two of them that first night in each other's company, but Serena could not bring herself to agree with Elston. All she could think of was that brief moment, under the trees as the Mountain Men drank and brawled.

When Milosh stood as her protector.

She had witnessed something beneath the hardened heart, something cracked and bleeding and feeling. Something that showed humanity he rarely showed otherwise.

And she did not miss the fact that he no longer bound her hands. There was a change in the air that she did not understand.

Beside Milosh and Serena, Elston rode on, whistling an unfamiliar tune. Soon they would descend from this small mountain, the last mountain between them and the flat plains and rolling hills of Southern Sindaleer.

The smell of smoke drifted over the wind, and loud voices sounded from the distance. Elston glanced around, his hand reaching for his sword. "More Mountain Men mayhap?"

Milosh drew in a sharp breath, his shoulders rising and falling. "We shall find out."

Serena noticed her hands glowing orange and hastily released Milosh's coat. She fought to regain control of her Gift, grateful that Milosh could not see her since she shared his mount. The leaves overhead rustled, the wind damp on her cheeks. Milosh slowed their mount's gait, pausing to glance through the heavy mist.

"Mayhap it's only the Guardians," Elston said, raising his sword.

"And mayhap not." Milosh drew his own, the sound ringing in the stillness.

The two continued to ride forward, the trees thinning as sunlight began to filter through. Shadows and the flames of a fire appeared in the distance, rowdy laughter drifting to their ears before ceasing. Elston glanced at Milosh and Serena with eyebrows raised.

"Halt in the name of King Thayer!"

Milosh jerked his horse's reins at the words, his shoulder almost knocking Serena off their horse. A scrawny man stepped out of the shadows, waving his sword in the air, the hood of his cloak pushed back.

Elston leaned forward, his eyes widening. "Twig? Is that you?"

The man peered at Elston and let out a laugh. "Elston! Who are these folks?"

Elston swung off his horse, clapping the man on the back. "A few... friends." He glanced at Milosh. "What are you doing here, Twig? Last I saw you, you were in some pub drinking to my health."

Twig laughed. "Oh, just with some of the old mates." He glanced up at Serena. "Now aren't you goin' to introduce me to your lovely companions?"

Milosh mumbled something under his breath Serena could not hear.

"Aye, of course." Elston gestured to Serena. "Serena, Twig. And, uh, Milosh... this is Twig."

"What kind of name is that?" mumbled Milosh.

Elston ignored his comment, turning back to Twig, his eyes alight with fun. "Now tell me, what brought you all the way down here?"

"Only traveling, Els. You and your company should join us for the night, take a load off them horses."

"I'd like that, Twiggy, if these two folks here wouldn't mind... Good ol' Milosh tends to like to journey until we're half-dead."

Milosh rolled his eyes at this.

Twig grabbed Elston, pulling him away towards the trees. "Splendid! It's goin' to be a fun night with ya here, like that time you dressed as a priest and those lasses—" His voice drifted away as they disappeared into a clearing.

"Mind?" Milosh asked, his voice dripping cynicism as he helped Serena down from their mount. "Why would we mind?" He lowered his voice. "But I swear, if Elston bloody tells these *friends* who I am, he'll live to regret it."

And so Serena found herself among five additional men, a jesting group whose teases and jokes had nothing to do with brandy or strong drink. Two campfires were lit, their mounts taken care of, and cups of mead passed around.

"Elston, old lad," called out one of the men. "Where have ya been?"

"Here and there, mostly there."

"So was it 'here' or 'there' ya picked up this pretty lass?" the long-haired man teased, tipping his cup toward Serena.

Milosh rolled his eyes as rowdy laughter followed the group as if he had spoken the funniest joke. Elston threw a wink toward Serena. "I think 'tis safe to say mates, I almost died at the sight of her, eh Springtime?" He glanced back at his friends. "Yes, lads, she was a breath of springtime in this cold world."

Raucous laughter followed at this comment, hands going to pat Elston on the back.

"Destiny save us," muttered Milosh from behind Serena, smoke drifting from his mouth as he took a drawl. "I am surrounded by bloody fools."

As the party heightened, Elston soon forgot about his two companions, lost in the absurd, ridiculous jokes of his friends and their silly songs.

Serena unrolled her blanket a good ten paces away from the party. A cool wind whipped the clearing in the wood, clear stars twinkling overhead in the blanket of darkness. A song about fair maidens was sung horribly enough to make even a small child cover his ears.

During the meal of soup and mead that Elston's mates had dished out for their new companions, Milosh stood in the background, smoking his pipe, watching. And through the chaotic song now, as night descended over the southern land of Sindaleer, Milosh's strong presence remained as he stood above her, his arms folded, staring off beyond the companions.

"Have you felt someone watching us?" Milosh asked, his eyes still on their companions.

Serena shook her head. "Nay," she whispered. *Enid?* her mind screamed.

Milosh glanced over his shoulder towards the darkened woods.

"Have ye?"

He took another drawl from his pipe, smoke drifting from his nose and mouth. Concern drew lines on his forehead. "Nay... mayhap not. But sometimes I cannot..." He stopped, shaking his head. "Forget I spoke. I am only imagining it."

As Serena curled under the blanket, she heard an owl soaring overhead, smelled the woodsmoke lingering in the air, and her lids grew heavy. She waited for Milosh to tie her hands as he had done every night since their meeting, to prove to these unruly new folk that he still had control over something, someone, to show that their thoughts did not matter but his mission remained the same.

But instead, Milosh stood by, smoke from his pipe curling to meet the sky.

Guarding.

Protecting.

Watching over the one who was supposed to kill him.

His eyes collided with hers. *Am I your prisoner? Are you conflicted?*

He held her gaze. *I mean what I say.*

Her mind flitted back to the Mountain Men and that moment Milosh chose to stay behind. *He's dangerous,* her mind argued. *Are ye going to trust this man who shoots arrows without thinking and cannot decide which side he is on? He's a dead man waiting to fall. He's going to take yer brother from ye. And Enid? What if it is her spying on us among the trees?*

Fear curled around her, but before she could think of some sort of reply for her weary mind, sleep crowded out all thoughts and she drifted into nothingness, Elston's companions' silly singing lulling her to sleep.

✗

Hunter hurried through the cold night, his face wind-chapped, his lips cracked. He'd passed through three villages already, helping smuggle out thirty seven lads in total, sending them to nearby Guardians who promised to take them across the border.

These were bigger, wilder villages then the ones Hunter had grown accustomed to. In one village he stumbled upon four lads in a circle around two mutts, cheering them on in a vicious fight. Blood from the animals coated the ground. "We're gettin' ready for war!" one of the lads shouted to Hunter.

Mutts were trained in Sindaleer for raids from Mountain Men, family feuds in other villages, or when merchants and pirates came to the south with intent to steal the young folk for slaves.

But the blood lust in the lads' eyes, cheering the mutts on to fight to the death, only made his stomach turn.

The south. The place of strife and big cities that reeked of dirt and grime of all kinds.

Night had fallen as he rode toward the seaport city. The moon stayed dipped behind dark clouds, and Hunter shivered in the chill, cupping his gloved hands up to his mouth, blowing into the leather, letting the warmth seep in.

He dug into his bag, drawing out the weathered map and holding up the faded paper. Reading the map proved almost impossible. Blamed darkness.

Through the faint moonlight, he figured out that the village he needed to go to stood to the east. Stuffing the map in his pocket, he rode on, the lights of the big city of Acwellen flickering in the distance.

Bron housed a few pubs where they sold mead, but the moral laws of the south did not match that north. Tales told with winks by the soldiers, who were called there when uprisings occurred, said Acwellen defined immorality. Lasses sold their bodies for scraps of food to feed their families, parents made deals with visiting merchants for money, trading their children to work on the ships as sailors.

Many never returned.

Hunter remembered one story told by a soldier

who was stationed in the south for a time. "I watched a woman eat a dead child because she was crazed with hunger. When I pried the body from her, she started screaming, 'he's dead anyway.' I still see her bloody face in my nightmares."

Hunter had no wish to go into the city, but it was the quickest way. Oh Destiny, his parents would die a second death if they knew.

Hunter shouldered his bow and quivers, urging his horse into a trot, crossing the road and heading for Acwellen. Once on the outskirts of the city, he slid off his mare, gazing around. Thatched cottages and buildings rose to meet the sky, the streets slimy with mud and gods knew what else Women slipped in and out of the allies towards brothels. The houses stood more like shacks, bare windows resembling a skull with its eyes prodded out.

Empty.

Death.

A man brushed by Hunter, the smell of alcohol and smoke on his clothes. "Watch it!"

Hunter ducked and hurried on, ignoring the man's dares to fight. He passed several street lads and lasses going through scraps that had been thrown from a window, and when he neared, his stomach twisted.

Putrefied meat. Resisting the urge to cover his nose, he crossed over the youngest child.

The wide-eyed lad whirled around at his approach. He opened his mouth, his front teeth black with rot. "What do ye want mista?"

Hunter reached into the pouch around his side.

His hand closed around some dried meat and one piece of copper Da had given him from his travels, hoping it might fetch some sort of deal if a trader found some worth in the piece.

The lad grinned. "Thank ye, mista!"

Hunter patted him on the back. "Ye share with yer friends here."

The lad grinned wider. "Aye, aye. These 'ere are me sisters. Ye can bet I'll share."

"Good lad."

Slowly, he turned away and went walking down the road past a pub, the living hell evident even in the dusk. Loud noises and a song from a pipe drifted through the doorway covered by a torn animal's skin. A woman threw her arms around a man in the alley beside him, laughing drunkenly.

For the first four years of his life, this had been home, but he failed to recognize none of it. As a child, innocence had blocked his eyes from reality.

And Hunter was no longer a child.

He pulled his hat lower over his ears, clinging tightly to his horse's lead rope. He couldn't fool himself. He'd come because this had been home, and mayhap, just mayhap, he wanted to see what home had once been for him.

He recalled life before the death of his parents, of playing in the sea, the taste of salt water on his lips. Serena would watch him from the shore, the water licking at her bare toes. He thought of the evenings when Da would come home from the wharf, the smell of Mam frying fish, of the stories Da would tell as they ate.

Legends were Hunter's favorite, and after their parents' death, he would make Serena retell them. Over and over and over so he wouldn't lose the last fragments of his childhood.

A soldier carrying a spear and circular shield stepped out of a pub. Hunter ducked into the shadows, holding his breath as the man passed. While unlikely he would be recognized, he knew that the soldiers journeying from Bron would be on the lookout for him, and he could take no chances.

Several more soldiers came out of the pub, their rowdy laughter climbing into the sour air. Their drunken words slipped into the night, too slurred to make any sense, but it wasn't the soldiers that sent icy tingles of fear down his spine.

It was the shields they carried—painted black with a white circle, marking them as soldiers from Bron. King's men. The ones sent to take the lads.

The soldier continued down the road, turning into an alley and out of sight. His horse knickered. Hunter patted the velvet nose before he mounted. Urgency pulsed through his veins.

Time was running out.

20

Enid whispered words into Serena's sleep now, as well as her waking hours. *Cease the line of King Thayer. His son has not chosen the side of the oppressed, thus we must rise. Kill him.*

Helpless, trapped in lies and deception as she had been from her birth, Serena longed to tell Elston, yet something held her back, a force more powerful than the need. A force that captivated her mind as she slumbered.

The force of Enid's words.

Two days after parting ways from Elston's companions, the jovialness of the night with them remained far behind in distant memory. The lightened mood had now dissolved, and Serena might have wondered if she had dreamed it all except for the fact that they had gained an additional horse for Serena that Twig fondly called "Kitty."

She drew in a deep breath. They stood on the last mountain, overlooking the valley, the coastal city of Acwellen, a haze in the distance beyond a rocky field. Salty air filled her lungs, and seagulls circled overhead, reminding her that they no longer rode in Northern Sindaleer.

Milosh and Elston each sat on their horses on either side of her, Elston humming a tune often used for the courtship dance after the harvest. "Do ye have a lass ye are courting?" Serena tried teasing, her voice strained.

"Nay, not yet, Springtime."

The further south they rode, the moodier Milosh became. As though his desire to find Hunter dimmed as they journeyed together, not as friends, but as companions who could at least tolerate the other's presence.

Serena could not help but wonder if Milosh held a second reason for this mission to the Southern lands.

"Milosh has been more sullen," she said quietly to Elston, watching the prince's straight back as he made his way on his horse down the hill nearly ten paces ahead. "He treats me less and less like a captive …"

"Aye, but you're a pretty lass. It must be hard to have you as a captive."

"Elston." Serena tried to hide her smile. "Ye are a good friend."

"Aye … " He gave her his side smile, though Serena could've sworn hurt flickered in his eyes before disappearing. "I still hold to my promise though, lass. I won't let that son of a prig hurt you or that brother of yours. I'm going to protect ya both. You need to see

Milosh for who he really is. You're trying so hard to protect Hunter, that you forget about yourself. If Milosh learned who you really are..."

"He's at war with who he is."

Elston threw her an exasperated look. "You'll see soon enough. I don't know why you stay with him as his captive anyway—we could both easily whip him." Then he rode on ahead passing the prince and riding on toward Acwellen.

She knew she should fear the prince, fear what he would do if he learned who she was.

But... Elston's flirting and Milosh's steel blade did not scare her. If she spoke the truth, the prince's protectiveness and her own confused heart, were the things that terrified her most.

As they rode, the prince continued in his quiet manner, his jaw set. Suddenly he stopped. Serena reigned in her horse, glancing in the direction of his gaze. "My mam lived in the village over that hill." He pointed in the distance to a tall ridge, and behind that a little forest of dark trees.

"Ye lived *here*?"

"For four and ten summers."

"What ... what happened to her, your mam?"

"She died before I had the chance to say goodbye. I received word from my village by way of traveling merchants last winter. I'd thought perhaps I would get to come down here one day and we would meet again." He drew in a ragged breath.

"How long ... since ye've been back?"

"Over five summers."

"I'm sorry."

"So am I." Milosh refused to meet her gaze. "I meant what I said before," he said quietly. "You are no longer my prisoner. I release you. You are free to return home."

"And my brother?"

Milosh set his jaw. "If I obey my father, I take the throne, Serena. Surely you see the difference that would make?"

"At the cost of lives?" Serena whispered. "Innocent lives? You said the rumors from the folk weren't true. Don't ye start now."

Milosh's hands played with the reins. "You don't know what it's like to hide, to pretend to be what you're not to stay alive." Then he nudged his horse onward, leaving Serena behind, staring at the lone hill in the distance where she could see the smoke rising from the chimneys of thatched cottages. Giant ponds surrounded the village, and men folk waded in the waters with heavy nets. Lasses beat at fur rugs and lads trained with wooden swords in the fields.

She closed her eyes, allowing the warmer sun of the south to seep through her tiredness, through the dirt caking her skin from their long journey, through the fear and trepidation.

Here had once been her home, the place where Mam and Da should have been buried, the place where she had been born, where she first learned that her Gift would be her downfall.

And as the ways of the world always seemed to go, her path had led her back to her roots, back to the place that she both dreaded and feared. She opened her eyes.

Destiny help them all.

✗

As Milosh rode away, his mind remained on Serena. Pity mingled with an unrecognizable emotion had mingled in her eyes.

But pity.

He drew in a deep breath, glancing back where Serena rode, her head down, her brown hair falling in wisps over her face. Ever since she'd followed him, he'd found that the defenses around his heart, the ones he'd labored to create, had weakened. His resolve to not let any folk see the struggles and weakness inside was slipping.

And that alone scared him.

He found, when he took the time to reconsider everything, that deep down he cared not that the lads were gone from the villages or if Hunter rescued them. He no longer saw Serena as his captive, and he no longer knew his own mind. He was a stranger, and everything he had ever thought in the last years was slowly slipping out of his grasp.

The truth stood before him. Hunter hadn't betrayed him. Not really. He'd only followed his convictions, which Milosh couldn't help but admire. He only wished he had that same courage.

Without pausing to think of his actions, he turned his horse's head, heading for the village that he had called 'home' in his youth.

"Oi!" Elston called after Milosh. "Where are ya going?"

His two companions followed, descending after him as he stopped short at the edge of the village, his heart roaring in his ears as his eyes landed on the stone cottage. Folk barely glanced at the travelers as Milosh slid off his horse.

His Mam's voice came back to him, her words haunting him from that day when the soldiers came to bring him to the castle. *Go with him, he'll train ye right, give ye a second chance. But don't forget killing isn't the answer. Violence never is.*

And his own voice filled his memory. *Nay. Nay. He is bloody dead to me. He is not my father. I'm going to stay here with you.* The pleading in his voice haunted him now. He had been such a lad.

He walked forward, slipping between two empty cottages to what had once been his own. The village was more deserted than he remembered, more sullen, older. Fewer children and women. No mutts barked in greeting as he strode forward.

The fur once covering the doorway was replaced with cobwebs. Milosh pushed them back with a gloved hand, stooping low as he stepped inside.

Mam, where is my da?
Nowhere lad. He's dead.

A lie he chose to believe until a soldier came for him, taking him away from his home, from the mother he vowed to protect, from the humble fishing village that was his one way of life.

And that was when the whispered rumors made sense, why the elders shunned and feared him since his birth.

They knew that one day, somehow, Milosh son of Thayer, would rise.

✗

The travelers galloped down the road off the mountain toward Acwellen. "How do ye expect to find any folk here?" Elston called.

"I'll know," came the curt reply.

And Serena knew he spoke the truth. Not much time would pass before they found Hunter if her brother still stayed close at hand, helping the guardians to sweep lads from the surrounding villages.

She pushed back a strand of stray hair, gazing at Milosh as he rode, his face sullen. He had not spoken a word as he'd remounted his horse at the village, his eyes glassy and hard. And for the first time, Serena began to see Milosh apart from the capital of Bron and the dark castle of the king. She saw him as more than a soldier and fighter, but as a simple, low country lad in a small cottage no different from hers.

And secrets. Always secrets.

Her heartbeat quickened. Should she let her own secret about the medallion break free? Could she dare trust him? She swallowed, her mouth dry.

As the city drew nearer, the sharp scent of sea salt and smoke from chimneys filled her nose, the billowing clouds staining the blue sky above the city.

As the hills rolled with tall grasses and the ocean's gray waters rose into view, nostalgia and fear pressed down on her heart as memories of the past flooded back. Home. This had been her home for the first nine summers of her life... a time so long ago that it could have been an eternity.

Many of the buildings stood as little more than shacks, the wood darkened from age. Fishermen and sailors sat on the docks, tipping up jugs of mead and ale even though the sun stood not yet high in the sky. Other men mended nets, the lads sitting on the beach with poles dipping into the rolling waves.

Milosh and his companions swung off their horses to walk the remaining way into the city. As Serena slid out of the saddle, her eyes remained on the water, the same water where she'd once played, where her whole world had existed.

Until everything she had known had fallen apart.

She shivered despite the almost spring-like warmth in the air, and drew her thin cloak tighter about her.

As she and her companions passed the ocean and the crashing waves toward the city, one of the sailors standing several paces away with a jug of ale, jumped off the docks, staggering over to her and offering her his hand. His shirtless chest gleamed with sweat, and his eyes glazed as he glanced over her body.

Serena stepped nearer to Milosh, and Elston moved to her other side protectively.

"Lassy, give me a dance." The man bowed, almost falling over his feet.

Milosh swore. "Get away."

The sailor's hair fell over his eyes, and he shoved the greasy strands back, grabbing her arm and pulling her away from Milosh and Elston before they could react. "Jest a dance," he slurred. "Jest one."

"Let. Go. Of. Her." Milosh drew his sword, the weapon slashing the air as the drunk's fingers closed around her arm. She winced, trying to tug free. His dirty fingernails cut the soft flesh of her upper arm, causing her veins to boil in fright and anger.

Her fingernails began to glow. *Nay, not now.*

"Ye heard the prince," Elston said, grabbing the man's arm.

The sailor spat again, glancing at Milosh. "Ye are the prince?"

"Yes. Let her go now before I cut you to bits." Milosh tipped the sword closer to the sailor's chest, drawing blood. The drunk jumped back, curses spewing from his mouth. "Ye cut me, ye no good da—"

"Curse the Marked! Of course I bloody cut you, and I will kill you if you do not get out of here."

Elston raised his small dagger. "Ye heard him."

The drunken sailor cursed again, turning on his heels and lumbering down the docks, talking to himself in another language.

Milosh drew in a sharp breath, sheathing his sword. Serena rubbed her arm, trying to allow the blood to flow.

"What did he do to you?" Milosh touched her arm, running his fingers over her skin. Serena shivered at his touch, but not from fear or cold. Mesmerized, she watched as he touched her torn skin, circling around the dots of blood seeping through.

"That looks nasty, Serena," Elston said, sheathing his dagger into his boot.

Serena withdrew her hand from Milosh's, pain and warmth mingling. "Aye," she whispered. "But I … I'm fine."

"Nay." Milosh tore a piece of his shirt and wrapped the tattered fabric around her arm, tying the cloth. "Nay. You're not. You're trembling."

Milosh glanced at her from the corner of his eye, and Elston winked. Lovely. Serena truly did not know if her shaking came from the sailor or Milosh's attention. Truth leaned on the latter, but she refused to believe that.

"This place is too dangerous for a lass," Elston grumbled. "You were daft to bring her here, Milosh."

"I had no choice with this foolish woman. She came because she wanted to find her brother. I did not choose it."

"Aye. Ladies get the best of ye, eh, Milosh?"

Milosh ignored this. "Let's find a place to sleep tonight that will be a bed and not the hard ground. Then tomorrow I'll find Hunter."

At his decisiveness, Serena's heart sank in her chest. She glanced into his eyes, but the protectiveness had vanished with his words.

21

Milosh helped Serena climb back on her horse while he and Elston walked on either side with their own horses, crossing through the city until they came to a decent-looking inn with white-washed shutters and a muddy entryway. Many houses surrounding it stood in shambles with unprotected doorways. Women scoured the streets begging for food.

Serena glanced away as a woman danced in the street, her bare belly and ankles displayed for passerby.

A child ran up to Milosh, begging for a piece of precious metal to use in trade. Elston bent down to hand him something from his pocket, but Milosh had already dipped into his satchel, bringing out a tiny piece that sparkled in the sunlight.

Serena bit back a gasp. What she'd first thought to be a dirty rock looked very much like gold, and little of that could be found in any region of the country. Milosh handed the precious stone to the little lass, patting her uneasily on her brown head and sending her on her way.

The child thanked him profusely before scampering off, her little feet disappearing behind the alleyway. Serena's heart dipped at the sight, and she bit back a smile before it quickly faded, her heart pounding with decision.

She had held off this talk long enough, almost hoping the problem would resolve itself and the medallion would somehow disappear like mist when the sun rises ... but that would never happen. Enid wouldn't allow it.

And neither would Serena's conscience.

She could no longer pretend Milosh would never find Hunter ... but would he hurt him? Would he throw her brother into a dungeon? Her mind now fooled her into thinking that he wouldn't, that the soft-hearted part of him was bigger than the monster raging.

Halfway into the city that crawled with men yelling curses and drunken sailors kissing loose women in alleyways that stunk of sewage and heavy smoke, Milosh stopped at an inn with a solid wooden door in the doorway. He helped Serena off her horse and the three travelers opened the door and stepped inside.

Serena glanced around the room, taking in the barren fireplace and rows of tables. No ladies dressed in naught but their underclothes stood about, only tired folk dipping chunks of hard bread into their cups, licking their fingers.

Some called out a greeting to the visitors, their

bows and weapons stacked by the wall and doorway, showing they came as friends and not foes, part of the common custom when entering a stranger's home. Milosh and Elston did the same, unsheathing their swords and taking off their quivers and bows.

The owner of the inn stood behind a dusty counter lining up his jugs of mead and ale. "Greetin's strangers! Yer not from around 'ere?"

"Nay." Milosh sat two pieces of raw gold on the table, no bigger than the nail of Serena's smallest finger. "Three nights."

The owner nodded, peering curiously at Milosh. "Down the hall. First door ye come to." He continued staring, looking back at Elston and Serena, then back at Milosh. "I feel as if I've seen ye around 'ere."

Milosh only pushed the gold further up the counter, took up the weapons from the front door, and nodded for Elston and Serena to follow him down the one hallway. Behind Serena, the chatter of the folk returned, rowdy laughter from one of the men echoing above the hub.

"Prince Milosh?"

The loud voice echoed above the hubbub of the folk, and Milosh swung around to face the voice. "Balder? Have you reached the south already?"

A tall man stepped out of the crowd, a fur cape draped over his broad shoulders. "That I have sire. We are returning to your father's castle with nearly a hundred lads to join his army."

"So little?" Milosh asked, but the question came weak.

"Aye. That lad you're after, that Hunter, he smuggled more lads than I thought he would." At the name of her brother on the captain's lips, a shiver raced through Serena's body.

Milosh rubbed a hand over his whiskered face, his eyes locking with Serena's before turning to Balder. "But still, I commend you for your work. Return home with the lads, and tell my father that I should be back in Bron in a month's time with Hunter's life claimed."

Elston muttered something under his breath about liking to see Milosh try, but Serena could not help but wonder if she detected a false tone of happiness in the prince's tone.

Balder nodded and wished Milosh an easy trip before turning to exit the inn. Milosh watched him go, his face hard, his jaw clenched. Then he opened the door to their room, allowing Elston and Serena to go in before him.

Elston threw himself down on the second cot by the one window. "This is where you will find me tonight."

"Nay, Elston. Tonight you must keep guard, and Serena will take that cot."

"Oi! You may be the prince, but I do have some say in what I do. *You* guard and I take the first cot. I chose to come on this journey."

"You did, but you also chose the responsibility."

"Nay, the only one who has to guard is the one on the king's mission...."

Elston stood and continued. "I will do as I please. I'm going to go find a drink and have some talk with the locals, and then I'm going to take a nap like any decent folk do after a long day's travel. And after that I may repeat it all over again." He opened the door, closing it with a dull thud.

Serena shifted from one foot to the other, glancing down at her dirt-stained fingernails.

"He's just a bloody son of a rat," Milosh muttered, going to stand by the window. "He knows I have no power over him. Not any real power anyway."

Without realizing what she was doing, Serena's hand slipped to the pouch with the medallion, reaching for the clasp. The gold weighed her down, more insistent, begging for the job to be done. Silence screamed in her ears. Then voices rose in chants in her mind, evil whispers that sliced her hope, circling her confidence.

"I ... I ... I must tell ye something."

"What is it?"

"I ..." Her hand of its own accord pushed the button through the clasp, her forefinger grazing the cold medallion. The whispers died down in one breathless moment.

"What is it?"

Serena sank down on the floor, her back pressed against the cold wall. "Many weeks ago," she whispered, "a woman came to me in the forest. She ... she had a Gift ... a terrible one."

Milosh knelt by her.

"She ... she called herself Enid and ... ordered me to kill ye."

Milosh remained silent, and she dared not look him in the eyes.

"I ... I wanted to refuse, but ..." Serena couldn't go on. She turned her head. "I believe there is war inside ye, as there is each one of us. And I believe that ye will choose the right side. That is why I cannot do what she commands."

The prince sat down beside her, his shoulder touching hers. Serena drew in a shuddering breath.

Milosh said nothing, the silence broken with his heavy breathing. When at last he spoke, his voice shook. Serena couldn't bring herself to look into his face. Her fear of him shook her courage.

"You could have killed me, but you didn't?"

Serena nodded, examining the dirt under her nails, his travel-stained boots, the whitewashed wall, looking anywhere but at his gaze which bore through hers with dark intensity.

"You had all the bloody chances in the world, yet you didn't raise a hand." He lowered his tone. "Did she threaten you?" Serena said nothing, and Milosh cursed. "She did, did she not?"

"Aye." She swallowed, the lump in her throat growing so it hurt to swallow.

"What did she threaten you with, Serena?"

Serena shook her head, holding her face in her hands. The pain of the past months flowed over her, relief and fear mingling with her twisted emotions. She wanted to curl up and sleep—sleep and never wake.

Milosh gently took her hands in his and lifted them away so he could look in her eyes. "What did she threaten you with, *mithrayo cartre*?"

Serena didn't know what language he spoke, but

the words rolled over her. She shivered, warmth tingling up her arms at his touch. "She ... said she'd kill Hunter."

"You would risk your brother's life for me?" He stopped, reaching up and cupping her face with his hands, lifting her gaze to his.

"I ... didn't think ye deserved to die. I believe in second chances," Serena whispered. *And, oh,* she silently pleaded, *don't look at me that way. If only ye knew the true me, if ye saw the Marks ... this moment would change forever.*

"But Hunter..." The words trailed from Milosh's mouth, his gaze glancing from her lips, then back to her face, searching her eyes as if trying to see her soul. "I was going to take him back to the castle...could have killed him...and still?"

Was going. Could have. The words of past tense were like healing powders to Serena's heart. He was no longer pursuing Hunter's life. He'd chosen his side.

Milosh's gaze, dark as night, caressed her face. Silence encircled them like a comforting blanket. Peace stole over her body. Everything would be all right in the end.

He leaned closer, his warm breath kissing her face.

The door flew open, banging against the wall. Serena jumped back from Milosh's touch. Heat flooded her face as she locked eyes with Elston.

Elston glanced between the prince and Serena, his eyes narrowing. "What are you doing?"

"That is not for you to ask," Milosh said, rising up and meeting Elston's gaze. "What are *you* doing here? I thought you went off to mope."

"I did, and I found who you're looking for."

Hunter. His unspoken name sent a thrill of fear and excitement through Serena. Milosh's face however, remained unreadable.

"Where is the lad?"

"Not where you can find him. I'm not giving him away for you to kill." Elston's hand moved to his sword. "This ends here. You're not going to harm either Serena or Hunter. I vowed to protect her and I will."

"Bravery looks good on you, but it's foolish nonetheless." Milosh's own hand clasped the hilt of his weapon. "This is ridiculous. Move out of my way."

Elston's eyes darted back and forth, and Serena could see the fear showing through his bravery. He knew he was no match for the known fighter, Milosh.

"Stop!" Serena jumped in between the two men. "Don't do this. We've lasted this far in each other's company."

"Aye, stop. There's no need to be fighting over me." Hunter stepped out from the doorway, pushing off the hood of his traveled stained cloak.

"Hunter," Serena whispered, running forward and pulling her arms around her younger brother. He smelled of sweat and dirt, his brown eyes bright as he surveyed Elston and Milosh.

"You reveal yourself at last," Milosh said.

Hunter nodded, but fear crept in his eyes.

"Nay," Elston said, drawing his sword and locking eyes with the prince. "I may act the fool, but I'm no dummy. You're not gonna hurt these two."

"You are a bloody—" Milosh began.

"Marked."

Serena gasped as the word slid from between Elston's teeth. His face paled as he realized what he'd said.

"I was going to say idiot, but that works too." Milosh paused. Silence roared in Serena's ears as realization crossed over his darkened face. He studied Elston. "Wait. You're not joking. You are serious?"

"Aye, dead serious."

"Elston, nay—"

But Elston cut back her words. "Nay, Serena. Let me do this. It is only right that Milosh knows." His eyes spoke what he did not say aloud. I am doing *this for you.* To reveal Milosh's true nature, to prove to her that he was dangerous.

Elston turned on Milosh, his face a deathly pallor as he assessed Milosh's reaction. "Aye, I'm Marked, Milosh. What say you now? Remember back in Bron, the missing Marked who you never found? Well, he found you instead."

Milosh said nothing. Serena could see his hands shaking. "Bloody he—" He stopped, glancing back at Serena. "You...you knew, didn't you? You knew that he was Marked?"

Serena glanced down at her hands as he continued to speak.

"You knew that we traveled with a Marked man... a dangerous man who was already arrested once. And why did you come, Elston? To help Serena? Or to plot against me?" His eyes met with Serena. "All along is that what it was? You know that I no longer treated you as a captive but as an equal...I began to trust you...I thought...I hoped..."

But he did not finish his words. Beside her, Hunter stiffened.

"Nay, it was not like that," Serena pleaded. "I came to help Hunter, to save him from ye and Enid...not to plot against ye. I wish I could have been honest sooner, but Elston's secret was his own to tell."

But her pleas did nothing to break the hurt and wrath from Milosh's face.

"Nay." Milosh turned to the door. "I cannot trust either of you. I hope you realize Hunter, that this journey was in vain, that my father already sent troops to round up the lads. You may have rescued a few, but my father obtained many more. Leave the country, all of you. Be gone. Next time, I may not hold back my wrath."

The door slammed shut as Milosh exited. Serena crumbled to the floor, her face in her hands. Numbness held back the tears, but nonetheless she continued to shake. Beside her, Hunter and Elston's faces showed equal paleness.

It was over.

She had failed.

"What do we do now?" Hunter whispered.

Serena glanced up at her brother, her heart shattered in more pieces than she could count. "What is there to do? I have failed. Enid will come and kill us all. She has plans to overthrow the king, and I have no doubt she will succeed...after she takes her revenge and kills...Milosh...after she does what I was ordered to do."

"She won't win. I'll make sure of that, Springtime." Elston kneeled beside her, but she backed away.

"Elston, ye should not have spoken so to Milosh. He was wrong...but we all were." Now the tears came, the flow like a river that could not be stopped. "Oh, it is all a confusion. No one is right, Elston. There's no simple answer...I hate this...."

She buried her face in her hands, breathing in the smell of dirt and sunshine from her palms. She tasted the bitterness of salt and regret on her lips.

And the sting of rejection continued to pulse with the remembrance of his anger...of his anger that made no sense yet made all the sense in the world

She remembered seeing him look out towards the village where he had grown and played. It had been the place where he had to abandon his mother for a father who only cared about making his son in his own image, a son to carry out his dirty work.

Serena knew the feelings well. She had battled mistrust and scorn all of her life. He may be a prince and she a simple Marked, but both in the end were right and wrong in so many ways.

Her hand slipped to the medallion that she longed to toss into the sea, to never set eyes on again, to toss the dreaded piece and be rid of it once and for all.

Beside her, Elston and Hunter remained quiet. She glanced up at them, hope lighting its spark. Resolution grew within her, heat pulsing in her belly. A smile curled at her lips despite the sadness.

"Elston, Hunter," she whispered. "I know what we have to do...if ye are willing."

22

Serena's hand closed around the gold medallion, her heart pulsing in her hand. The wind dashed over the waves of the sea, the salt air teasing her tangled hair. Hunter and Elston stood on either side of her, their shoulders brushing hers.

"Are ye ready for this?" Serena asked them.

"Ready or not, you're doing this anyway, aren't you?" Elston replied, a hint of playfulness in his voice.

Serena drew in a deep breath, letting the wind expand her lungs. With a whoosh, she let it out. The drums of her heart thumped against her ribs. She stepped forward, the cold ocean water lapping at her bare toes.

"Do it, Serena," Hunter said from behind her. "We can't go back now."

Nay, she could never go back. She'd come too far already.

And with that thought, she let the medallion fly.

The gold piece soared through the blue sky, the glint of the sun burning her eyes. The accursed medallion seemed to hover, for but a moment, in the air before a wave swallowed it in its murky depths.

A beautiful weight lifted off her shoulders. While her heart remained shattered in her chest, she for the first time in many months, felt freedom. To let go of the medallion, to be free of what had held her captive, to toss it away in the depths of the ocean; the act of it all, almost took her breath away.

She glanced back at Elston and Hunter with a sad smile.

"And now we wait?"

Serena shuddered, her hands beginning their orange glow. "And now we wait."

✗

They waited on the edge of the beach, the sand stretching on for miles. She had started a fire, not hesitating to use her Gift. The three of them shivered in the cold despite the flames, listening to the lap of the waves crashing on the beach.

Enid would come for her. Whether that be today or tomorrow or the next.

Fishermen with poles on their backs, headed home. Sailors lit their own fires down at the docks, too far away to hear, but the orange sparks glowed in the distance. Ships stood anchored in the distance, no doubt full of goods to trade.

Serena wrapped her arms around herself, trying to ward off the bite of the wind. Where was Milosh?

She could see his eyes, the black curls that always got in the way. His darkened skin, his almost black eyes, each setting him apart from the lightly tanned skin and eyes of the Sindaleer folk.

She remembered the way he studied her, as if she fascinated him, as if she was worth watching.

Serena shook her head.

But now he was gone and he would never return.

Serena pulled her knees to her chest. The stars popped out of the velvet sky one by one, and the moon hung over the oceans' waves, climbing to its rightful place in the inky blackness. She swallowed, closing her eyes, soaking in the calm before the storm, the peace before the war that would surely come.

It wasn't supposed to end this way.

In the fairy tales, she and Milosh would marry and live happily ever after, and have children and the Marked would be free. But this wasn't like the fairy tales of old. She and her brother and Elston stood alone, and they would fight alone.

"What was that?"

Serena opened her eyes, glancing at Elston. "I didn't hear anything."

"Nay, wait. I hear it too." Hunter jumped to his feet, drawing his sword.

Serena strained to hear what the others heard but only the call of the wind and waves met her ears. However, the hair on the back of her neck prickled and fear gripped her heart nonetheless.

She clenched her hands into fists, fighting for faith and courage. Her hands began to glow orange, smoke drifting from the tips of her fingers.

Then she heard it, the light noises as someone treading softly through sand and grasses. The sickening sweet scent of lavender met her nose.

"She is here." Serena swallowed, her strong words hiding the fear that collided with the anger inside. Her heart hammered. She drew in a gasp of air, fighting for control.

Elston brandished his sword, Hunter his bow. Together they faced the tall grasses, the thump of Serena's heart nearly drowning out all sound.

"I see that you do not take orders well." The words bounced off the silence.

"Show yerself!" Hunter called out, fitting an arrow to his bow.

"So brave and so foolish," Enid replied. "Serena, why did you disobey? Why did you not kill Milosh when you had the chance? Why is my medallion in the depths of the ocean?"

"Because unlike ye, I believe in second chances." Serena's voice quivered, her hands brightening as she spoke.

"Nay, because you are weak. I was wrong about you, Serena. You are like all the other folk, too afraid to fight for justice, to rage war. You find yourself more content at peace even though every day folk die at the hand of King Thayer."

Serena refused to reply, grasping for courage or bravery that slipped further and further away.

And they waited, the three of them in the darkness, for the sorceress to strike. But like a serpent she too waited, biding her time, drawing them in.

"Do you know what happened to me?" Enid's voice said. "I watched my husband and son, who was no more than ten summers, die at the hands of King Thayer. I watched as King Thayer's men ravaged our country, killing those whom he found to be a threat. My son was no threat. He was just a lad who wished to fight, to be seen as a hero. And he was a hero, for he did what you could not do, Serena. He died fighting evil.

"And you will die tonight, but you will not die a hero. You will die a slave to the king."

"It depends what you call a hero," Elston replied, his voice surprising Serena. "Step forward, Enid. We're ready."

And suddenly Serena saw her.

Her eyes locked with that of the sorceress, Enid's flaming red cloak standing out in the night sky. The ocean's roar crashed in her ears.

Serena let out a gasp, falling to her knees. Pain tore through her senses, grasping for her sanity, ripping through thought and feeling. She cried out, but no sound escaped her mouth. Her head connected with the wet sand.

Voices whispered. *My curse will now fall upon you and your brother. You have failed. I have more on my side than you imagine. The time of the Marked is at hand and you have missed your chance.*

Darkness surrounded her, mingling with the agony. She grabbed her head, rocking back and forth. She silently pleaded with the madness but still it came, like a torrent of waves, one by one, pain attacking her.

White spots danced in her eyes. Hunter screamed, miles away and far from her grasp. Serena fought her sanity, but the darkness pulled her in deeper. No thoughts but the pain surrounded her.

She pleaded with it to stop, to cease, to allow her to breath. Her chest begged for air.

Death began to claim her. Enid would win.

Lights collided with the darkness. She gasped for breath.

She wouldn't die a hero in her country's eyes; she wouldn't become a part of the legends. But she had fought for the little bit of good left in her world, and to her, that was all that mattered.

The pain began to vanish, bit by bit falling away.

She smiled. Sweet peace assaulted her, driving away the madness. Sleep...she needed to sleep.

Was this the end? Mayhap...and it was a better ending than she could have thought possible.

23

"Nay!"

The roar brought Serena's heart from her chest, back to her senses, back from where she lay cradled in darkness's sweet arms. She opened her eyelids, fighting for control, fighting to lay eyes on the person whose voice shook her away from the black death welcoming her.

What had happened?

Where was Enid?

The ocean crashed against the beach, roaring in her ears. She realized she lay on the wet sand, soaked to the skin. Her head swam. The world around her moved at a dizzying rate.

She sat up, exhaustion nearly pulling her back into the darkness. Her eyes locked with a figure battling with Enid on the beach. "Milosh..." His name fell from her lips, and she blinked.

Nay. He had left.

He was gone. He was not on the beach with them, fighting their battle. He had abandoned them.

But nay, there he fought with Elston, the clash of steel echoing in the night. "Milosh..."

Hunter lay on the sand beside her a couple yards away, his eyes closed. The battle raged around her.

Elston struggled, his sleeve ripped and dark with blood. They would not win, not against such a powerful Gifted.

Serena tried to stand, her legs trembling beneath her. The world around her swam. She closed her eyes, waiting for the motion to cease.

Warmth coursed through her body. The sand sank beneath her as she took a step forward. Her head ached from the curse Enid had placed over her and Hunter.

Serena's hands clenched into fists as she willed her Gift.

Milosh fell to the ground, his head in his hands, screaming in pain. Serena's body shook. Warmth mingled with hot rage as the prince writhed on the ground.

"Nay!" Serena ran forwards. Her heartbeat rammed against her ribs, threatening to break free. Her stomach churned and she thought she would vomit.

Her body convulsed as a flood of fire and smoke swirled from her hands both beautiful and deadly. She cried out as weakness threatened to throw her to the sand. Her hands raised, she aimed at Enid, praying Destiny would guide her.

Enid's gaze locked with Serena. "You've already been cursed, Serena. You are all going to die."

The four of them were down on the wet sand now, death a breath away. Serena lifted her head as the pain dulled.

Enid turned her gaze to the prince as he tried to stand. "Weak... so weak," the sorceress whispered. "I promised Tirich that I wouldn't use my Gift, but there's something sweet about us here. I couldn't resist…" Milosh opened his mouth to cry out, his body writhing in pain.

Serena attempted to rise, but weakness stole her breath. She fought to summon her Gift. Panic caused every nerve in her body to tremble. "Nay! Nay!"

The glow in her hands brought only weak smoke.

Unless Enid died, the curse over her and Hunter would consume them both.

"Do you see your lass now, Milosh son of Thayer?" she heard Enid say, holding Milosh's face in her pale hands. "Do you see her wrists?"

In the darkness, Serena could see his eyes dart to hers.

"Do you see her wrists?" Enid repeated. "Marked. You were lied to, betrayed. She is just like me. A Marked, hated, hiding under your very nose."

Milosh's gaze found Serena's. Sorrow. Hurt. Pain.

"I'm sorry," she mouthed.

She again tried to will her Gift, to feel the warmth of fire course through her veins, but her weakness stole her breath. Enid turned, her eyes locking with Serena's. *You have failed. You will always fail. He doesn't love you. You are going to die for a lie.*

Serena turned, waiting for the pain, but none came. Out of the darkness, a hoarse cry echoed across the sandy beach. Serena watched, tied in horror to the ground as Elston rose from where he'd lain on the ground, his own sword gleaming by the light of the moon.

Serena screamed. The world paused to take a breath. The lap of the waves against the beach mocked them.

Elston ran forward, raising the sword to plunge into the belly of their attacker. Enid turned, her own sword drawn.

"Are ya prepared to die?" he called.

And before Serena could scream his name, Elston plunged his sword into the sorceress at the same time Enid's own weapon took its blow.

Serena's heartbeat counted the seconds.

One

two

three.

The sorceress slid to the ground, red liquid staining the sand. The light faded from the Marked lady's eyes.

Strength flowed through Serena's veins.

Life.

The curse over her and Hunter snapped.

Elston glanced at Serena. "It's over, Sunshine," he whispered; then he fell to the sand.

"Elston!" Bile rose in Serena's throat. Her body shook as she slid down beside him. Her hands cupped his face, his skin cold beneath her fingertips. "What did ye think ye were doing?"

"I..." Elston tried to smile, but blood pooled from his mouth. His hands weakly clasped the sword in chest as he tried to sit up. "I... I... promised... in Bron... to.... return the service..."

Serena shook her head, her vision blurry. "Nay..."

He coughed. "And... Milosh... tell... that son of a rat..." The words slipped out in a whisper. Serena pushed back the damp hair from around his eyes. "He's... not... his... father..."

The eyes of Elston dulled. His hands grew cold as his spirit vanished, abandoning this world for the next, a hint of a smirk still playing around his mouth.

24

Serena leaned against the cold walls of the inn. Hunter lay in the cot several paces away, his face peaceful in sleep. He had woken once since the fight with Enid, his wounds unable to break his spirits, though exhaustion stole his body.

Milosh sat with her as Hunter slept, his arm bandaged, the crust of blood around his wounded lip visible in the dim light of dawn.

He'd barely spoken.

As they sat in the inn, as she glanced down at her hands stained in the blood of her friend, numbness stole emotion from her body. When she looked into Milosh's face, she saw the defeat. He hadn't said why he came back, what had changed his mind. His face remained rigid in the dim light of morning, unreadable.

"Elston wasn't supposed to die," Serena whispered at last. "It was supposed to be me."

"Nay, you are wrong... it was me... it was always supposed to be me." Milosh turned, his leg brushing hers as they locked eyes. The pain his face held almost took her breath away. "Elston was right, I am everything Thayer ever was. I am what Thayer wished for, a replica of himself."

"But... ye came back..." The words slipped from Serena's tongue. "And... after everything... ye are still here... after you know I am Marked."

Milosh drew in a sharp breath. "I was wrong to leave."

His words held truth, and Serena knew not what to say to this.

"I was wrong," he repeated. "I was scared, and for the first time I realized I needed to choose a side, whether for good or for evil. I had remained on the bridge all my life, doing what benefited me, and for the first time that was far from good enough. You were brave to choose a side, as was Elston and Hunter."

Serena swallowed, her eyes searching Milosh's face as he glanced away, his jaw clenched. "When ye said I was no longer yer prisoner, and when ye came back... when ye came back to help us... ye chose yer side. Ye being here now... ye chose yer side."

Milosh searched her face. After a pause, a small smile played on his lips. "I still cannot believe it... A Marked?"

Serena nodded, fear settling like a stone in her stomach. She pushed back her sleeves, exposing the ugly tattoos that stained her wrists.

Milosh swallowed hard, his gaze impossible to read. Silence collapsed around her as she waited.

"What is your Gift?" he asked finally, his voice tight to her ears.

"I can make fire." Exhaustion stole strength from her body, but she allowed warmth to flood her body, tiny tongues of fire curling into her palm. She drew in a shaky breath, afraid to meet Milosh's eyes, afraid to see him abandon her again.

"Do you know why I came back?" Milosh said at last as the small flames licked at the wood. "When I left, I rode back to my village, and there I thought of my mum. There was something about being back, here in the south. It brings back a powerful remembrance of her, almost as if she is still alive."

Milosh swallowed. "She once told me that we all have gifts. She told me that after I watched my village burn a Gifted alive."

"We don't all have Gifts," Serena began, but Milosh held up a hand to stop her flow of words.

"Nay, not like Thayer sees. I cannot make fire, but neither can you wield a sword. We are all dangerous in our own right. Each gift is powerful, my mum said... But seeing the power of the Gifteds, I had to agree with my father. Fire, Serena, that's dangerous... but I sat in my old cottage and I could almost feel my mum's arms around me.

"I remembered her sacrificing so much for me, her bastard child with a quick temper. I remember her giving me the last bit of food and her going hungry. I remember her bidding me farewell as I abandoned her.

She knew without me there, unmarried, sick, and with only the harsh village folk, she wouldn't survive the winter. But still she bade me go to Bron, the rightful prince of Sindaleer, to one day reign, to change the course of Sindaleer's future." Milosh's eyes hardened.

"When I came back here to the south, I thought of her, of her sacrifices for me in my life, how she wished for me to have a good life. And I thought of her telling me that each Gift holds power... of how my father's gift as a warrior has destroyed lives, how my own gift for fighting could have destroyed.

"And I thought of my mum, and the power of her love. And you better bloody believe me, Serena, love is powerful, more powerful than any gift." Milosh drew in a sharp breath, his fingers brushing her's. "Love brought me back to you..."

"And Elston's love for me made him lose his life," Serena murmured, a tear slipping down her cheek.

"Nay. He gave it away." The pad of Milosh's thumb brushed away the liquid. "He gave me a second chance with you."

Serena let out a low laugh. "I'm Marked, Milosh. I'm dangerous."

"You're bloody right, you're dangerous." Milosh tipped up her chin. He did not smile, but his eyes softened. They warmed her like hot, liquid fire. "I am sorry for everything, Serena. *Everything.* All my father and I did. I am not who I want to be."

"No one is," Serena whispered. "I'm not."

"Then... Do you want to learn who we are together?"

Before she could answer, his lips covered hers.

✘

Hunter and Milosh laid Elston to rest on the bed of logs they had hewn and bound together. The ocean lapped playfully at the small craft that would soon take Elston away forever.

They had bound a cloak over his body to hide the wounds, his sword laying clasped in the hand at his chest. Milosh's jaw remained clenched as he glanced back at Serena. "What do you wish to say?"

"Farewell, Elston," Serena murmured, the words catching in her throat. "Marked and lover of stories and legend, ye gave the ultimate sacrifice. We thank ye."

Milosh nodded, his body rigid. Together, he and Hunter pushed the raft into the ocean, the water up to their waists as they helped Elston begin his final journey. Serena's hands glowed, warmth and pain coursing through her.

In a nearby tree, a small circle of peeled bark still smoldering, lay engraved a simple X. She swallowed, her hands closing into fists, the light extinguishing. The raft bobbed in the calm water, pulling further and further from land until it remained but a memory.

Elston, the Marked and Gifted Storyteller, was gone.

Milosh caught her eye.

What do we do now? Her heart longed to ask. *What will become of me... of us? Who are we?*

She no longer recognized herself as the lass she had been back in the small village of Aedre, yet neither was Milosh the fiery prince proclaiming hell and death, nor Hunter the childlike brother she remembered. They had changed, while the world around them remained the same, both beautiful and ugly, cruel and dark.

Enid had promised her that more forces were at work, ones stronger than the sorceress. What did this mean for Sindaleer, for the many battles that lay ahead? And when Milosh became king, who would accept her, a Marked and Gifted?

Folk already saw Milosh as a threat to the country of Sindaleer, and she would only greaten that divide.

Milosh's wet hand slipped around hers, and a peaceful warmth swept around her, begging to draw away all her fears. She wanted to lean into Milosh, to marry him. She wanted to close her eyes and see that all was right with the world.

But nay, Elston now lay in the depths of the ocean. He had given all of them a second chance at life, and she could not waste hers and neither could Milosh

25

Three Months Later

"Ready to brave this hellish crowd?"

Milosh glanced up at the soldier and nodded. Already the mobbing had begun. The jeers and taunts of the folk could be heard half a mile away. Behind him he could see the village of Aedre, burned by his father months before.

"The mobbing and riots began not long after you left," one of the soldiers told him. "Yer father thought it best to show 'em what it means to respect."

Milosh drew in a deep breath. "I'm ready."

The men at his side drew their swords, surrounding him as they entered through the gates of Bron. "They're protestin' fierce today," yelled the soldier in front of Milosh.

"Why didn't my father throw some in the dungeons?"

"There were too many. He nearly lost power."

And died at their hands.

The kingdom would have crumbled had not his father's advisor remained loyal to his post, ordering the soldiers to drive the folk back into the streets. Milosh swallowed as they entered the inner city of Bron, the jeers and boos of the folk rising around him, taunting him.

"Go home, son of a rat! Go back to the country ya father was from!"

"Stay and die!"

"You'll die as he did."

The sour smell of rot and filth filled the air. The soldiers pushed their way through, the large procession of guards encircling him tighter. Around Milosh, on the walls of homes, hung heads on stakes... his father's doing... or the folk's?

What had happened to this part of the country while he had been away? He ground his teeth together. What had Thayer done?

"It's hell on earth," a guard called above the noise to Milosh. "Absolute hell."

The crowd pushed in closer, but the soldiers waved them away with their swords. "Any folk who get near here aren't going anywhere without a fight."

The castle of Bron rose in his sight above the many heads of the folk as they pressed on. They paused at the gateyard of the castle where a hundred soldiers lined up, their bows in hand as if ready to aim into the angry crowd. Milosh pushed through into the gateyard, his heart pounding, sweat trickling down his neck despite the fact that winter still loomed.

In the castle, a heavy silence descended as he entered. The kitchen grew quiet, filled only with whispers and stares at the prince who had been away to get lads and returned empty-handed. Selwyn, his father's advisor and most trusted servant, hurried to him with outstretched hands. "My Lord, we have long awaited your return—"

"Yes, I know. I bring no lads, but I heard that my soldiers returned with many good ones?"

"Yes, yes, my lord. Strapping lads for this horrible business. They await your command. I myself, sire, have been awaiting your return as I held down the castle. It's a nasty, nasty business out in the city."

Milosh only half listened to Selwyn's prattle. "Am I crowned then?"

"Yes, yes. The old ways of Sindaleer have long since passed. The throne is yours at the death of your father. The folk wait for you to place the crown—"

Milosh pushed past Selwyn, hurrying up the corridor and the stone steps to his father's chambers. It had come to this.

As he entered, his heartbeat throbbed in his chest. He was here. After four months of travel and pain, after years serving his father's nefarious motivations, he was here.

His hands curled into fists. Here he stood in the same place his father had stood but two weeks past, the

man who had been this country's downfall. He turned to
the door leading out into the balcony.

Serena.

He ached for her—for her laugh, for her gentle
smile. She lightened his heart in an instant, and made
him feel stronger than he knew he was.

He remembered the evening after Elston's
burial, holding her hand, sitting by the ocean, listening to
the lap of the waves against the beach. She had looked
up at him, full of trust and sorrow and pain, and he found
that more than ever he wanted to hold her, to take away
the darkness she had experienced at he and his father's
hand.

"I should have..." *Been a better man. Stood up to
my father. Taken death as was my right.*

"Milosh," Serena had interrupted, and he
savored his whispered name on her lips. "I'm not going
to ask ye to change the past—no one can. We can only
change the future... And Elston, he gave us that chance."

Serena looked down at their intertwined hands.
Her fingers glowed, warming his skin, illuminating their
scars. "Elston... before he died, he told me to tell ye that
yer not yer father." Her eyes met his in the darkness, and
she reached up to place her hand on his heart. The light
shone like a star, through his thin shirt and to his beating
heart.

"He was right, ye know," she spoke softly.
"Ye'll never be yer father. Yer father has had many
chances to change and yet he doesn't. But yer heart's
still beating, and ye have that chance and I think ye will
take it... She paused. "Nay, I *know ye will.* And so did

Elston. "

"I can't go back with ye..." she had repeated over and over, as if to convince them both. "It's not my time. It's yer's. The folk need ye, and I know ye will be a good king even if they don't."

"Milosh." The voice dragged him away from the past, but it was not Serena standing before him.

"Hunter! I thought you wouldn't come." The lad stood taller, his hair pulled back with a leather thong, a hint of a beard above his lip. He looked older, healthier...whole.

"I got your message from my Guardian leader," Hunter was saying. "And I brought some boys with me. They'll help ye gain trust with the folk."

"I'm glad you could come, lad."

Hunter bowed. "I am honored."

"Have you heard from...?"

"Nay, but she said she would send word later... when it quiets down, when the Gifted have a place."

Milosh's hands shook as he placed them on the cold, gold crown on the stand by the balcony door. Outside, the mob had silenced as if holding their breath, waiting for King Milosh to step forth, to replace the former murdered king.

"I'm doing this to carry on the work of those before us."

Hunter nodded, swallowing hard.

"Are you sure you wish to do this with me?"

"Aye... together."

"They're not going to receive us well, Hunter. They knew my father, and they want me dead. They wish for nothing more than to see me on a stake like the one they gave my father. I feel something more sinister at work than that of the sorceress, more battles with the darkness. Are you ready to fight, lad?"

Hunter nodded again.

"Ready?"

"Oi! Who ye tryin' to convince?"

Milosh laughed hoarsely, drawing in a deep breath. The crown settled on his head, the weight and the cold both comforting and frightening.

His own time had come. Whether he felt ready or not, it was here, upon him.

Milosh pushed open the balcony door, and together they stepped out.

✗

Serena stood at the edge of the angry crowd, her black cloak wrapped around her, the hood pulled around her face. The hisses and boos of the folk circled around her, the air vibrating with heavy tension.

Her breath caught in her throat. Milosh, the newly crowned king of Sindaleer, stepped out onto the balcony with her brother. They stood so tall despite the anger of the mob before them. The two of them against the opposition of a country.

Many would call them foolish, but Serena felt sure she had never seen two braver souls.

Milosh did not know what he would face in his reign. Enid had threatened that a force more powerful than that of her own Gift, stood on the horizon. The darkness had not died with the sorceress.

But then, darkness does not begin and end with one person. It is a continual, pulsing threat, capable of destroying lives.

Serena cas her eyes back one final time at King Milosh and Hunter, their faces grim and proud. She knew Milosh would fight this coming darkness bravely. In the end the greater weapon would endure, and love is the strongest of them all.

Tears threatened to spill, but she held them at bay. She had to be brave and strong. Time would pass. She would be back.

Soon Milosh would change the laws Marking the Gifteds. Soon.

Behind her she could still hear the folk, and she closed her eyes, leaning against a building. When she had told Milosh after Elston's burial, that she could not return with him and Hunter, the sorrow on his face had sent her heart into a million shattering pieces.

"I cannot," she had said, trying to remain firm. They had been preparing to travel back to Bron, and Hunter was planning to join the Guardians, to seek out the darkness that Enid had warned was coming.

Serena remembered stepping back, her hand leaving his. Cold air had swept between them, and it had taken all her resolve not to step back. "The folk will accept ye even less if ye marry a Marked. The time of the Marked is in the past... and mayhap the future... but not now. I can't do that now. I plan on staying in the south."

The firmness in her voice did not match that of

her heart.

"Serena... don't. I cannot fight this alone." The pleading in his voice had almost been her undoing, and she refused to meet his gaze.

"Nay, ye don't need me. Ye have to do this alone, Milosh. It's yer time—not mine. Mayhap one day soon... but not now."

Serena swallowed back the emotion closing her throat as she remembered hugging Hunter farewell, of seeing the two she loved most, ride away from her. And now they stood in arms reach, so close yet never further away.

She turned, leaving the city of Bron, the castle, the village of Aedre behind. The mob could still be heard from behind the city's walls. Dark clouds formed over the sun, shutting out its bright light. The brown mountains of winter mirrored her own deadened heart, but spring would come.

The mountains would not remain dead forever. This was only a season.

Serena untied her horse from around the small sapling and mounted. She refused to look back as she urged the mare south bound. The cold wind pushed back her hair, flowing through, drying the tears she hadn't realized were coursing down her face.

Every season has a beginning and an end.

She would be back.

Kara Linaburg

If I can stop one heart from breaking, I shall not live in vain.
Emily Dickinson

.

Dear Reader,

Maybe you're confused. *Why the second edition, Kara?*
In 2019, I wasn't expecting very many people to read
this little novel, and while it by no means made any
milestones, it went far further than I'd anticipated.
People actually read it!

I wasn't expecting to try and make writing a
career, but now, as of 2022, I am in school for editing
and publishing and am contracted with a publisher for
another YA novel. How much time can change! This
being the case, I wanted to give *The Broken Prince* an
updated, refreshed look that doesn't use stock photos
everyone recognizes.

I also got feedback about Milosh, and that some
had felt I'd played off Stockholm Syndrome, which was
by no means my intention. Milosh is a flawed character,
but by capturing Serena, I never wished to portray him
as manipulative, narcissistic, or Serena's love for him
being based on dependence or sorrow.

Therefore, if you read *The Broken Prince* in
2019, you most likely see some slight scene changes in
this updated edition. I did this in order to clarify
Milosh's character progression, and to show that he did
choose the light. This is still a flawed story, but
hopefully you saw some good changes.

It was so much fun to dive into Sindaleer again, and to try and deepen the story and make it an easier and much clearer read. I hope it brought you a little light as it did me. And now, a note from Kara in 2019...

✗

We all have our demons.

Mine has always come in the form of anxiety. I have had anxiety about my self-worth, anxiety about life and death, about social gatherings... but often for no reason at all.

My anxiety rose to the point a few years ago where I didn't want to leave the house for anything or anyone. Even family gatherings or talking with friends left me sweaty, nervous, and on the verge of an attack.

All through High School I would often be in tears, sometimes unable to breath, shaking, trying to control something that was controlling me. Battling between depression, self-hate, and a deep-rooted anxiety that refused to leave, I was exhausted mentally. I was sick and tired of this living hell that had me trapped since before I was eleven years old.

The written words have always been my way to communicate, my breath of fresh air, a way to cope and to find answers, and I found that Milosh and his struggles mirrored my own. We were different, yet the same. I have always struggled by labels the world had slapped on me, by my circumstances and past defining me, by feeling alone in the battle. Like both Milosh and Serena, I wanted to live free, to be who I wanted to be with nothing holding me back.

I'll be honest—I'm not good at faking it, and the world can be cruel to people who wear their hearts on their sleeves.

I wrote *The Broken Prince* because I felt alone in the fight, and I didn't want anyone else to feel the way I did. I wrote because I needed to, because I couldn't keep the words inside.

For so long I allowed my struggles and past regrets to define who I am and who I will become. For so long I was afraid to be transparent, afraid of rejection if I ever was.

But, in between writing, I learned this:

There is a God who knows no limits, who loves you for you. You can laugh at that if you want. You can tell me I'm naive, but I'll just tell you that He's the reason I'm still alive.

We are not defined by what we call ourselves or the limits we put on ourselves, but by who HE says we are.

God says we are loved, that the darkness will not win, that we can fight. He says that we are strong, that we are brave, that we are beautiful. He says that it's never too late, that we are worth fighting for.

I write because of that. I write because what I feel doesn't matter, does not define me.

This book was one girl's aching heart poured onto the pages, a girl who ached for answers, ached desperately for others to see that there is such a thing as second chances, and to choose to live freely because of that.

We are all desperately, deeply, painfully broken.

But there is hope in that brokenness.

I sincerely hope that reading this you have enjoyed Milosh and Serena's journey. Their brokenness mirrors my own, and it is such a joy to share them with you. They are probably more real to me than any fake human has a right to be, and you holding this book in your hands holds so much excitement for me.

Keep fighting the good fight, friend.

You are loved.

Never forget that.

Many Thanks...

Oh, I'm finally at this point. Wow. Already?! There's so many people to thank and hug and talk about. Sadly, if I thanked every beautiful soul who has made my writing dream come true, it'd be another book, so I am truly sorry if I miss out on mentioning you here.

Writing *The Broken Prince* has been a very long journey, one of ups and downs and tears and triumph and pain, but there have been people who have stuck with me through it all.

First and foremost: My Heavenly Father. Thank you for giving me reason upon reason for living, for telling me my brokenness will one day be healed, and for calling me Yours. It is because of You I am able to write, to live, to breathe. Without You I could never put pen to paper.

Many thanks to my family who love and support me no matter what I do. Korin, thank you for being my second brain, listening to my many rants, and helping Milosh (and me!) find a path to healing.

Charles Thomas, Josiah, and Jeremiah who will read my book even if they say otherwise. You are dead wrong boys: every book should have a little bit of romance.

Kailin for being my fellow romantic heart from an early age. It's so much fun having you "ohhh" and "ahhh" over mushy parts in stories with me.

And many, many, thanks to my parents who didn't think I was (too) crazy when I dropped out of college to try and make it as a writer. Thank you for choosing to homeschool us, for loving us, and for sticking through with every battle.

My cousins, aunts and uncles and grandparents: All who are too vast to name and would take way too many pages if I tried. I love having a big family and I love you. Your support over the last years means the world to me.

Alyssa, one of my biggest cheerleaders, best friends, and sister surely separated at birth. Thank you for your prayers, long talks, and for being my friend through it all. I could never have had motivation without you! Here's to more years ahead, lots of Florida visits, and family vacays.

Thank you to Jess for promising to buy my book all the way over in Australia, for your loving support, long distance video chats, and long letters. You are so strong and I admire your faith. You make me want to be a better human. Your prayers have literally meant the world to me, and hopefully when this is published I can say I've hugged you in person.

Thank you to my editor Rachelle who took my poor little novel that desperately needed work, and made it look good. You saved me from making a truly horrible ending and killing off a truly valuable character.

Thank you to Tasha. There's nothing like connecting over something as amazing as Tolkien and finding we had even more in common. You're one of my favorite penpals.

And to all my friends, supporters, and all those who have ever read my novel before it was in any decent shape and said it was good. I love you (even if you lied ;).

And to you.

For reading.

Thank you.

Thank you.

Thank you for following Milosh and Serena's journey, for holding this book in your hands. It means so much to me that you have read *The Broken Prince* to the end.

The Human Behind The Book

If you combined Lucy Ricardo, Jo March, and Tonks, you would have Kara. Queen of awkward, writer before she could properly spell, and maker of imaginary humans, she is passionate about creating characters that display beauty in brokenness.

When she's not being a mad scientist in the kitchen or daydreaming about her next adventure, she loves to connect with readers. She lives in West Virginia where country roads always take her home.

You can feel free to stalk her website and find her other published works @ www.thebeautifullybrokenblog.com

The journey continues...

Turn the page to read a preview from the second book
in the *Crowned Duology*

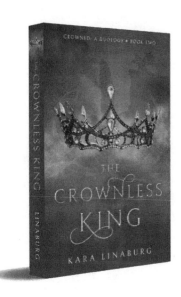

Available on Amazon

Prologue

*"**W***hy did you abandon me?"*

"Because I knew I needed to make my choice."

"What choice was that?"

"To choose between the lesser of two evils." She gazed into the face of her captor, his dark eyes probing deep into her soul, seeking to devour her sanity.

"You realize the consequences of your actions, do you not?"

Her hands curled into fists so tightly her knuckles popped. "Death."

"You speak as though the idea holds little power."

"I do not fear death, only the pain of it."

Admiration flickered in his brown eyes. "Few maidens could say the same."

"Few maidens have experienced death as closely as I." She wanted to close her eyes, to vanish to a time where beauty collided with her world and the black stood far away. "I have seen the darkness. I fear nothing but the pain now, and even that will not stop me."

"You had a place with us. You should not have left."

"I was a puppet to your lusts for power."

"You were my warrior."

"I was an assassin."

"I was fair to you."

"You were never fair."

Her captor rose, pain rising in his eyes. "You betrayed us—all of us."

His voice held heartfelt emotion that she longed to believe.

But she had played his game long enough. She knew his intentions and the thoughts of his heart. He would have the folk eat his words without question, digest them, and allow them to consume their sanity. The Manipulator spoke and they believed his poison.

And she prepared for death to swallow the breath from her lungs.

Also from Kara Linaburg...

"Poignant... visceral... Linaburg has crafted a story that will arrest your attention from its beginning all the way through to its soaring conclusion."
Brian McBride, award-winning author of "We the Wild Things"